JOHN CHARLES REEDBURG

# CRACKS OF LIGHT

VALOROUS
BOOKS

Published by valorousbooks.com

ISBN: 978-1-7365535-0-3 (Ebook)
ISBN: 978-1-7365535-9-6 (Paperback)
ISBN: 978-1-7365535-2-7 (Hardback)
ISBN: 978-1-7365535-1-0 (Audiobook )

Library Control number: 2021901802

*For Momma.*

# TABLE OF CONTENTS

# PROLOGUE

*My family household consisted of the five of us: my mother, my mom's drug habit, my momma's bipolar disorder, that mysterious light in my room, and me.*

CHAPTER 1

# THE FIRST TIME
# 1 SAW THE LIGHT

As a kid, I was never afraid of the dark; it was The Light that scared me. It didn't come from phobias, or flashbacks about fires burning, lightning, or anything involving electricity; what I dreaded was a radiance that manifested and emerged from the dark.

I was four years old when I first saw The Light. I was in my bedroom closet when a speck of brightness, floating in a sea of darkness, first seen out of the corner of my eye, got my attention. It bounced against me, hitting my nose and my face, forcing me to grab at it and swat it away like a firefly. I was never successful— not that day, not ever. I could tell from how it moved that it had a mind of its own. It came every night afterward, whether or not I was sleeping. I always knew when it had passed through, because my room would smell like jasmine and orange-flavored candy and the temperature would drop to an unbearable, penetrating chill. The air I exhaled was as white as a ghost.

One night, when I was nine years old and close to falling asleep, a cloud of light appeared from the shadows of the ceiling and hovered over my bed. The brightness had grown. It was no longer a spot of radiance shifting in the darkness, but a brilliant cluster of energy the size of a crystal ball. My dark room was the night sky, and  The Light was a sphere resembling many tiny exploding moons. And it was calling out my name. Although The Light had never spoken to me before, when it did it sounded like a girl my age. She wanted to know if I was sleeping.

"Demetrius, are you awake?"

I squeezed my eyes shut and pretended to be asleep. Maybe if I played the Jedi mind trick and planted the opposite suggestion in its thoughts, The Light would be persuaded to go away.

"Demetrius," the voice said. I felt my bed shaking. "Are you awake?"

"No."

The voice giggled. "You're funny. Do you want to hear a secret?"

"No."

"Don't you want to be my friend?"

"I didn't say that," I said, now trembling.

"How about we play a game?"

"No, thank you."

"So, you lied. You don't want to be my friend."

My eyes opened. "I didn't say that."

I heard a crackling noise. Suddenly, the dark face of a young girl poked through the portal of light and came toward me until both our noses were close to touching.

I froze.

Cracks of light spilled out through the outline of her face. Her glare had a power that seemed to move right through me, and her frown became a smile as soft as my pillow. My mind filled with questions, and her wink held all the answers. I didn't have to say anything more. She pulled back into the portal with a look on her face that informed me she knew me.

The Light vanished.

I screamed at the top of my lungs: "Momma!"

*  *  *

In the beginning, the shades stayed lowered to protect me from the outside world. Like the walls of my mother's womb, they kept me safe, like a caterpillar inside a cocoon. No matter how hard I tried, my imperfections never allowed me to become a butterfly; my failures were only a part of being human. Momma told me I was an old soul that been here before; I had been blind to The Light and had lived for months inside the darkness of the vessel that carried me. I survived the blackness with no signs of life except for those thumps from the heartbeat pounding against my chest, like an enraged animal that wanted to escape. A tentacle attached to my stomach was like a cord from the universe that fed my existence—until one day, when a portal of brightness appeared and pushed me toward the end of a shadowy tunnel, toward The Light. One of my mothers from a past life told me that The Light had its own world, and if I ever got in, I would experience fear. The Light was an energy, albeit in a different form.

\* \* \*

The year was 1983; I was born into poverty as a black boy named Demetrius. My mother was Olivia Jordan. We lived on the third floor of the Park Arms Apartments, in an area of Los Angeles called Hyde Park. Our building was a four-story lime structure that crawled with ignorance, pain, and unfixable, broken families. If busted couches in front of buildings stuck out like a sore thumb, Park Arms was the black eye of the neighborhood. Our two-bedroom apartment would have been a perfect fit if Momma and I were cockroaches.

During the day, my room was a place to do homework and watch TV. When it was time to go to sleep, it became a dark emptiness that had part of its space filled with a dresser, a closet, and a single bed. And there, hiding in the shadows, were poster-filled walls plastered with powerful superheroes who never saved me.

# CHAPTER 2

# HE TOLD HER TO BEAT ME

I had never told Momma about The Light, and for as much as I screamed for her that night, I couldn't tell her about the girl whose face poked out of The Light because Momma didn't believe in ghosts. Was the orb (and the girl) an alien, a spirit, or a figment of my imagination? The consequences of figuring that out were too great. Momma never behaved like other mommas. Maybe this was because she was fourteen when she had me. Maybe it was her height; at four-foot-eleven, she was only three inches taller than me by the time I was nine. Momma was the big evil sister I never had.

She dyed her long dreads into the colors of the rainbow—with Kool-Aid. She had lost weight and had welts on her arms from drug use. Momma had been pretty before she got hooked on dope, although she still had a lot of boyfriends. She called them "sugar daddies." They bragged about how she looked better than the girls in rap videos. She was never too cute to be mean.

As for telling Momma about The Light—well, I couldn't.

One time, when the orb came into my room, I ran into hers, my heart beating fast, screaming, "Momma, there's something in my room. It won't go away!"

She sat on her bed in her bathrobe and didn't move.  As steam from the running shower poured into the room from the crack under the bathroom door, Momma stared out the window in a daze.

"Momma, did you hear me?"

"Go back to sleep, Demetrius," she said, and didn't turn around or break her gaze. "If you don't, I'll have him deal with you when he gets out of the shower. I know you don't want that, do you?"

"No, ma'am."

"That's a good boy."

I had to face The Light to avoid the terrible pain Momma's other half so often inflicted. A part of me wanted him to die in that shower.

Momma called him "Geppetto." He pulled her emotional strings, but he wasn't my father or my mother's boyfriend—Geppetto was Momma's bipolar disorder. He became a part of her life before I was born. She hoped and prayed he would never be a part of mine, but he stuck around, and she hated him for it.

Momma described him as an elderly, sweet-faced Italian man with lined bifocals and a thick furry mustache the color of train smoke. He wore black trousers and a brown dupioni silk vest, a cream linen shirt, and a leatherwork apron as worn as the callouses on his fingers.

She loved how his eyes were the same color as the ocean.

I called her manic moods "The Blues." The Blues made her despise anything that made me happy, even if it was something that Geppetto told her he wanted me to do.

She told me someone had to step in as my dad; black fathers didn't exist for black boys. Momma thought a white man should have taken his place, so she thought Geppetto did a better job, even though he was just an imaginary man that lived in her head.

Geppetto was the co-parent in a single-parent household. Whatever he said, she did, and he told her it was okay to beat me.

\* \* \*

I remember when Geppetto had my mother punch me in the eye and lock me in the kitchen closet. The cabinet was small, dark, and cramped, and reeked from the damp mops turned upside down inside it, propped against the wall to dry.

Lightheaded and thirsty, I waited for signs Momma remembered I was there in the kitchen closet, that she was ready to forgive me, but there was nothing—nothing until a voice emerged from the darkness.

"Do you want something to eat?"

I opened my eyes wide.

"Are you hungry?"

A speck of brightness appeared and grew from blackness. It was The Light. I nodded at the glowing ball. The girl's smiling face formed on the surface of the orb.

"Don't worry. I got you."

The closet door opened. A giant chocolate cake and a large glass of grape juice were on the kitchen table. My eyes grew big with excitement. "Oh man!"

"Now, do you want to be friends?"

I was too hungry to respond. I charged at the table like a madman and devoured the cake, using my hands as utensils. Who had time for forks, knives, and spoons? I downed the juice with a mouthful of dessert, emptying it all into myself. With a full stomach, I belched. I forgot The Light was still there.

"Do you have any manners?"

"Excuse me."

"We're friends now, right?"

The orb moved in circles around the shadowy kitchen. I contemplated an answer, but before I could respond, the sound of footsteps neared the kitchen. A finger reached across the wall, turning on the light switch. Momma saw me there with icing on my hands and face. The orb disappeared.

"What you doin' eating up all that cake?! That food was for company, boy. How do you think he'll feel about that?"

"Momma, it wasn't me."

She beelined toward me, smacking me across the face. I fell to the floor, crying.

"I'm tired of you lying. You're a little, lying, worthless bastard. I better not ever hear you talking that way again. Now get your black ass back in that closet before I beat it off you."

The closet door closed on me. No, Light girl, we weren't friends.

10

CHAPTER 3

# THE UNIVERSE'S PUSSY

F unny thing—Momma knew the Bible well.
　　She was the daughter of a minister whom
she only referred to as Pastor. Although we
had never met, I called him Granddaddy Pastor, but
most people knew him as the Reverend Dr. Reginald
A. Jordan, founder of the African Luminous Body
of Christ Church in the affluent black neighborhood
of Ladera Heights, minutes from our lower-class
neighborhood in Hyde Park. Pastor's organization was
said to be a cult, which was the truth. During the
1970s, he trained under James Warren Jones of the
Peoples Temple. Jones was known for leading a mass
murder-suicide in Guyana, in which his 918 followers
drank cyanide-poisoned Kool-Aid. Pastor vowed to
follow in his footsteps.

Momma didn't want me involved with Pastor or his religion. She lived on the street, pregnant with me, until she moved in with Aunt Charlene. Charlene was her eldest sibling, and the first to run from the cult. Charlene despised Pastor for the way he treated his kids. She also blamed him for Grandma Mabel's death. The day she died, Charlene left.

With little help from anyone outside of Charlene, I never understood why Granddaddy Pastor never helped us. While he lived a wealthy life, we wallowed in  poverty. I didn't care what Momma and Charlene said about the man—all I wanted was a better life as a family. We all could've discovered how to become normal. I mean, I was already okay with being a fatherless child. Momma said it was in the universe's plan for everything to work out how it did. She thought it was best Pastor wasn't a part of our lives.

Her favorite quote from the Bible was a line from 1 John 1:5 that said, *God is light; in him, there is no darkness at all,* which, according to Momma, meant there was a little part of Satan and God in all people, so if you focused on the good, you would never succumb to the Devil. So, anytime I went through dark times, my imagination was the shine that kept me from being destroyed. "The Lord's will is the Lord's way," is what Momma always said. I guess that meant the higher power up above was a stubborn person, as most men are.

For some reason, Momma hardly ever took me to church, and the one time she had, it was to have me baptized. She told me it was her way to make sure I was protected. She declared, "The supernatural will always save you. It'll help you before anybody else." Anytime I went to church, I felt loved and accepted, and something inside me made me feel better than I had ever felt. I wanted to go more often, but Momma would never take me. I hated that.

She had odd theories about God. One night, sitting next to me in our living room, my mother told me she had proof God was a woman. I was intrigued, so I asked, "How do you know God is a woman?"

She paused, smirking. "How do I know?" she said, giggling like a schoolgirl with a secret.

"How you know, Momma?" I replied, like she was about to show me a magic trick.

"Let me show you," she said, an all-knowing gleam shining in her eye like she had every answer in the world. She took me to a nearby open window and pointed to the sky. "If you look out deep into space and focus your eyes past the stars, you can see the universe's pussy. That's where the world comes from."

"For real, Momma?" I said.

"Yes, baby. It is for real. Keep focusing," she said.

So, I stared deep into the heavens and saw the shape of something that outlined the stars. I didn't know what it was. At nine years old, I had never seen a pussy that didn't have fur and whiskers.

"But, Momma, I still don't see it," I said.

"Give it time, baby." She placed her arm around my shoulders to encourage me. "Take a deep breath and count to ten. It'll come. Trust me," she said.

I counted to ten, and there it was. The universe's beautiful pussy, giving birth to billions of stars. I was so astonished I froze. The only word I could get past my lips was, "Wow."

That evening, we watched the stars until it was time to go to sleep.

# CHAPTER 4

# AUNT CHARLIE

Tall, high yellow, freckled-faced, and pretty, with the same eye color as Momma and me, Aunt Charlene was my favorite person in the world. She called the spots on her face cinnamon sprinkles and joked about being a big sugar cookie in pumps. She nicknamed me Honey Bear. Whenever she came over, she brought cooked food and a sassy attitude for Momma to match.

Charlene had a mouth slicker than my mother's, and a way of putting her in her place. Anytime Auntie talked badly to Momma, my mother got quiet, soaking it all in. I enjoyed watching, but holding my laughter behind a blank face was no easy feat.

This one time Aunt Charlene came over, she looked in the fridge and said, "This baby needs food, honey— real food. Not no dang junk food and no goddamn fast food, bitch. Every time I'm up over here, there ain't nothing in the damn fridge. It ain't even enough crumbs to feed a roach. Honey Bear ain't got no new clothes, or a good momma to raise him. He's a growing boy, sweetie. Do us both a favor—find your life and get yourself together, bitch."

Momma had enough. "I know he's a growing boy. I'm not stupid."

"Act like it."

"Act like what?"

"How do you have the nerve to sit around and watch TV like you don't have something better to do, bitch? The world can't revolve around the boob tube, you know."

"We're not kids anymore, Charlie. I don't need you to come telling me what to do."

"Girl, you better thank Jesus's black ass and hope that's all I do. Name's Charlene, honey. Charlie died in that fire a long time ago. Respect Mother for who the fuck she is and who she always will be. Get that right, and I might thank you. I don't need to be welcomed, fish."

"Whatever, Charlene, I don't need your advice right now."

"Girl, please. There's a lot you don't need. Those crayon dreads are one."

"Ain't nothing wrong with my dreads."

"You been taking your medicine?"

"Don't like the way it feels."

"Shooting yourself with that stuff?"

"I'm a big girl, Charlene."

"Answer the question."

"I'm good."

"Ollie?"

"Whatever I choose to cope with my damn self is none of your business, Charlene."

"Oh, girl, I've got your business. And I know you've been hitting this boy."

"No, I haven't."

Auntie looked Momma up and down. "Yep, you have. I know how violent you get."

"You don't know me."

"I know your ass is crazy when you ain't taking your medicine." Charlene yelled from the kitchen, "Honey Bear!"

I responded as if I wasn't peeking and watching the entire time. "Yeah?"

"Get in here, mister."

I came darting in. "Yes, Auntie."

"Let me see your arms," Charlene requested.

I raised the sleeves on my shirt. Momma stayed nearby, watching nervously. It wasn't the first time she'd had something to hide.

"That ain't necessary, Charlene. You always in my business," Momma said.

Charlene glared at Momma. "This is my business." There were a few fading bruises on the outsides of my upper arms. Auntie grabbed my hands, caressed them for a moment, and then requested I tell the truth. "She's hitting you again?"

Reluctant to respond, I looked over at Momma, watching her gently shake her head and mouth the word *no*. Charlene reminded me I didn't "have to lie," so I looked her in the eye and told her, "Momma didn't hit me. My bruises came from this bully at school."

She looked at Momma and then back at me. "We're going to have to do something with that boy, okay?"

"Copy that," I said.

"Go in the living room. Let me talk to your momma."

"Okay." When I left the kitchen, I stayed near the doorway, out of sight, soaking in as much of what they were talking about as I could.

Charlene gave Momma a stern warning. "Touch that boy 'gin and I'll call Child Services my damn self. Doubt me if you think I'm playing."

Momma was afraid, and Charlene looked like a big beige bird towering over a worm. She rolled her eyes at Charlene. "Nobody scared of you. I'm not hitting my son."

"Stick with that lie if you want to. But don't hit him again. Be here with more food next week." Charlene yelled for me, "Honey Bear, come walk Auntie to the door. Need to pinch them cheeks before I go."

Momma stood in the kitchen, glad to see Auntie walk out.

# CHAPTER 5

# FRY JACKS, BLACK EYES, AND PAPAYA JAM

My best friend was a Belizean girl called Natalie who lived in my building. I sometimes called her "Nats" for short, and her mom was the reason I loved the smell of sweet papaya jam on salty, warm, and fluffy fry jacks in the morning. Fry jacks, a traditional breakfast in Belize, were fried pieces of dough, and Mrs. Peters was the best at making them. Since my momma couldn't cook, Mrs. Peters would hook Nats up with extra treats to share when we walked to school—fresh fruits, fry jacks, bacon, hard-boiled eggs, toasted tortillas with sugar and butter, and if it was a lucky day, Natalie would bring out enough homemade tamales for both of us.

Natalie had a thick Creole accent that made her sound more Jamaican than Central American. Despite her African ancestry, Natalie's deep caramel skin; long, black, wavy hair; and dark doe eyes made her look East-Indian, another part of her heritage. She had a way of always keeping her beautiful head of hair hidden beneath a ball cap. I never understood why I was attracted to her. A big fan of Michael Jordan and the Chicago Bulls, she was a tomboy who always dressed in her big brother's basketball hand-me-downs. She didn't like "girl clothes," and seldom wore a dress.

The first time I saw her, I swore she was a boy. We met in the first grade after her folks moved into our building. She was in the hallway with her mom.

I could tell she was in my grade, so I was like, "What's up, homie? What kind of toys you have?"

She looked at me and frowned, "I'm not a boy, and I'm not telling you!"

Mrs. Peters smirked, "She is a girl, son. Her name is Natalie, and yes, you can come over and play anytime."

"Mommy, no! He is dumb. I don't like him," Natalie said.

"Hush, little girl. Be nice."

"Sorry, Natalie. My name is Demetrius. I didn't know you were a girl. I like your shoes," I said.

"Boy, bye. I can't," she repeated.

"Natalie!" her mother shouted.

I walked past them feeling bad until I looked back and saw Natalie making a funny face. We both laughed.

We became friends a couple of summers later when she joined my team for a game of kickball at school.

And by the way, I didn't call her Nats because her name was Natalie, but because she hated gnats or anything with wings that stuck to her face, which could have gone for ants and cockroaches, if they knew how to fly.

Nats had a brother named Herman, a sixteen-year-old basketball kid who turned into a thug after he joined a gang and dropped out of school. Mrs. Peters knew he  was bad news when he started selling drugs and robbing people. The only parents we had were our mothers.

Natalie's mom was entirely unlike mine. Her mother loved her for any and everything she had done. My mother punished me for the things she assumed I did. One time, Momma gave me a whooping because she thought I hid her syringe. Geppetto needed to use the needle. He had type 1 diabetes and would have died without his insulin. She punched me in the face and accused me of trying to kill Geppetto. The next morning, Momma apologized. She didn't even remember what happened. When I left the house, Natalie snuck me into her bathroom and covered my bruised eye with some of her mother's Maybelline before we went to school. Mrs. Peters had no idea we used her makeup, but it wasn't the first time.

Whenever Natalie and I walked to school together, which was only a couple blocks away, kids would tease us about being boyfriend and girlfriend since we hung out so much. I never knew there was a rule that said a boy and a girl couldn't be friends without going together. Even though I had a crush on Natalie, I never was sure about how she felt about me in return. How would I even know anything about being a boyfriend? I had seen it done on television, and it seemed like being a boyfriend was cool. Theo from *The Cosby Show* made it look good until he split up with Justine. Jack Tripper from *Three's Company* made it sound complicated because he had too many girlfriends. Steve Urkel from *Family Matters* was never able to get with Laura, and I didn't want to be like him.

If Natalie were my girl, I would be the type of boyfriend Alfalfa was to Darla in *The Little Rascals*. Being around her always gave me goosebumps, and I knew if she ever kissed me, every hair on my head would stand at attention—sort of like how Alfalfa's hair stood up whenever Darla kissed him on the cheek.

I wondered if any of my mother's sugar daddies kissed her the same way I wanted to kiss Natalie. I wanted to be her sugar daddy. I would have done anything to make her my sugar momma. Walking to school with Natalie was the best part of my day.

CHAPTER 6

# FRIENDS AND SISTERS

23

C harlie wasn't her only sibling; Olivia had an identical twin named Lydia, who promised they would always be together, no matter what kept them away from each other. Their father believed Olivia to be an old soul sent from God, despite him always punishing her for the smart mouth she had. She was his favorite outspoken daughter that everyone called "Ollie." He wanted Lydia to be more like her sister. Lydia was less bright and witty and would get sad from time to time. It was something that came from their daddy's side of the family.

The twins often dressed alike in taffeta dresses. They kept their long hair up in shiny barrettes and pretty ribbons, each girl using separate colors to help others tell them apart. Every night before going to sleep, they would tell each other what they wanted to be when they grew up. Olivia would stand up on her bed and place her right hand in the air, her left hand over the chest of a nearby Barbie doll that Lydia held up. Olivia gave her speech to the room while her sister and the toys watched.

"Tonight, from this bed, I, Olivia Jordan, swear on the life of this white Barbie doll that I didn't want my momma to buy, that when I get big, I will become a superhero with strength more powerful than Wonder Woman. I will have curves like Pam Grier, and my sister Lydia will be my sidekick."

Lydia disagreed. "I'm no sidekick. I'll be Eartha Kitt when she played Catwoman against Batman in her leather suit." She then stood on the bed with an oath of her own. "I, Lydia Jordan, swear on the life of this white Barbie doll that I didn't want my momma to buy, that when I get big, I'll be the prettiest beauty queen in the world, and you can be the prettiest one on the planet."

"Ain't those the same thing?"

"I don't know."

* * *

One time, Olivia looked Lydia in the eye and told her, "When we get big, we gonna do everything together, like get married, and have babies. Shoot, we'll probably even have houses next door to each other."

"Like them white folks on TV?"

"Yeah, but …" Olivia had a wild imagination.

"But what?"

"I want twenty kids."

"Twenty?"

"Yep. And they'd all be twins like us. And all girls; I hate boys."

"Child, you better hush. I hate them, too," Lydia chuckled.

Olivia wondered, "Where do babies come from?"

Lydia shrugged her shoulders. "Santa Claus."

"Momma said they came from a stork."

"Would we need different storks?"

Olivia smiled. "Maybe."

The girls laughed.

Olivia held out her pinky. "So, friends forever?"

Lydia held out hers. "Yep, friends and sisters."

The twins interlocked their fingers to signify their vow.

When one twin was in trouble, the other would take up for her. Once, Pastor came into their room steaming and blowing his hot air. He went in hard on the girls.

"Which one y'all heathens ate meat out my crockpot?! Mouth all watering for oxtails got me looking in the dang thing, and all I see is beans. One of y'all little heathens will get it!"

For some reason, Olivia couldn't stop laughing.

Lydia nudged her to be quiet, but it didn't help. "Ollie, stop it, you're gonna get us in more trouble," her sister whispered.

But Olivia kept rolling. She had the chuckles.

"Ain't nothing funny, little girl. You ate the meat out of my beans? Had them cooking the whole day. Seasoned just right. But I know what this is. Spare the rod, spoil the child." Pastor took off his belt, folded it in two, and held the strap by its fastening ends before popping the opposite inner sides of the leather together to startle the girls. Olivia had stopped laughing, but it was too late. Pastor was ready for the next beating. "If one of you is smart, you'd tell the truth to save yourself. Who ate my tails?"

Lydia stepped forward, "I did, Daddy. I ate your oxtails all up, and they were good, too. They're right here in my belly, mm-mm delicious." Lydia rubbed and patted her stomach like she was stuffed full.

Pastor smacked her across the face with his backhand.

Olivia watched, terrified, not knowing what would happen next, as Daddy glared and snarled at her identical half. "You little, high yellow, piss-colored bitch, you ain't nothing but Satan's spawn. God told your momma not to have you, but she didn't know no better. I'd kill your behind dead right now if I didn't have to go to Hell to do it. Damn heathen. Ain't worth shit."

It was hard for Olivia to step forth, but she did. "Pastor, I ate your tails. Lydia didn't want me to get in trouble."

Pastor smacked Olivia to the ground, and she fell next to Lydia. "You are two of the most lying little bitches I ever seen. I bet y'all gonna be whores when y'all grow up. Ain't worth shit. And since neither one of y'all don't wanna tell the truth, how about I whoop both y'all asses?"

"Daddy!" Lydia cried.

"Don't go hollering now, you little bitch. But before I begin wearing y'all little yellow asses out, I want y'all's opinion about this scripture I'm going to talk about Sunday. Think it'll be good for first service, but ..." Pastor stopped mid-thought. "Wait a minute, I need you two little bitches to hike up your dresses, pull down your drawers, and bend over while you're at it."

The girls followed instructions, and like always, Pastor continued without letting up. "Don't worry about y'all showing your little bootie meat. I've seen it before. Maybe it'll remind y'all what you took out my pot, heathens."

Olivia begged in tears, "Daddy, Pastor, please, please don't whoop us."

"Don't worry. I'll take the blame. I'll let him know I took the meat. I won't be scared, I promise," Lydia whispered to Olivia, but Pastor overheard.

"It doesn't matter who takes the blame. I'm still going to whip the Rottweiler's shit out of both of you. You little bitches; crying is not gonna help." Pastor picked up a Bible and started beating the girls with his belt on their bare buttocks. He read scriptures out loud, and took turns giving his daughters their divided abuse, each blow in rhythm with his words. "Matthew chapter four, verse sixteen. 'The people living in darkness have seen a great light; on those living in the land of the shadow of death a light has dawned.'" The beating stopped. "Little hussies know nothing about that. Need to start calling you heathen bitches One and Two."

After the beating, Pastor had the girls sit next to each other on their sore backsides and recite chapter one, verses five through nine from the first book of John as they held hands. The twins simultaneously repeated what he taught them out loud. Pastor called out verse numbers, and the girls would respond.

—Verse five!

—This is the message we have heard from him and declare to you: God is light; in Him, there is no darkness at all.

—Verse six!

—If we claim to have fellowship with him and yet walk in the darkness, we lie and do not live out the truth.

—Verse seven!

—But if we walk in the light, as he is in the light, we have fellowship with one another, and the blood of Jesus, his Son, purifies us of all sin.

—Verse eight!

— If we claim to be without sin, we deceive ourselves and the truth is not in us.

—Verse nine!

—If we confess our sins, he is faithful and just and will forgive us our sins and purify us from all unrighteousness.

—You, heathens, confess your sins of lying and stealing meat out my pot.

—Yes, Pastor.

—Good. That's what I wanted to hear. Now let the Lord wash away your sins. Say 'Jesus, wash away my sins.'

—Jesus, wash away my sins.

Splash! Pastor drenched the girls with a bucket of red liquid. It might've been blood, or it might not. The twins cried and screamed in horror. Pastor's usual coldhearted scowl cracked into a dubious smile. "It ain't the blood of the Lord, but it'll do. Y'all take a bath before y'all carry your little asses to bed. Heard me?"

"Yes, Pastor," they said simultaneously.

Their father left.

Lydia looked at Olivia, unable to believe what just happened. "Do you think it's real blood?"

"I don't know, Lydia. It looks like blood."

Lydia stared at the puddle of nearby liquid in addition to what was on her body and clothes; she stuck a couple of fingers in the red pool before taking them out and smelling them. "It smells like pennies," Lydia said.

Olivia stood up. "I hate pennies." She held out her hand to help Lydia off the floor. "Let's get cleaned up."

\* \* \*

When their older brother Charlie came upstairs, he saw the girls in the hallway headed for the bathroom. He was appalled they were covered in what looked like a gallon of blood.

"What happened?"

"Pastor used Jesus's blood to wash away our sins," Olivia replied. "Do you think it's really blood?"

Charlie touched some of the liquid on Olivia's face and rubbed it between his fingers. "I think it's blood." Charlie became agitated. "Momma!"

"She's not here," Lydia said. "She went to Bible study."

"We have to come up with something to stop Pastor. We have to let Momma know too."

"Do you think Momma will help us?" Olivia asked.

"If it's a part of God's will, she'll help us," Charlie responded. "Get cleaned up, then come to my room."

# CHAPTER 7

# WHAT THE PIG TOLD THE WOLF

31

Whenever I went into the hall close to Momma's room, I had to be careful so she didn't know I was there. If I didn't, I became every victim who took too long to get out of the water in the movie *Jaws*. The sight of her coming out of her room was like seeing a shark fin. Her hallway was her ocean. I never blamed her for all the times she ate me alive.

"I know Labradors are smarter than you," she once said with a tone sharp enough to torpedo any hope I had left in my day. "Think money grows on trees? Frugality is a nectar you need to drink. You can't buy that with food stamps, boy. It's expensive."

"I didn't mean to eat the cake, Momma. The Light made it happen."

"Sorry." She shook her head. "Your excuse is not gonna cut it. Why you make me hurt you so bad, Demetrius?" She hit the light switch on the wall and headed toward me. "LIGHTS! OUT! I'm the only one paying the bills around here."

I ran from the now shadowy hallway to the kitchen. Momma came after me, ready to pounce. I positioned myself behind the nearby table, out of arm's reach. She kept trying to circle around.

"I don't want you to hurt me."

"That's what the pig told the wolf. Shame on you for being a bitch. You are so weak. I need to whoop your ass to teach you. Go to them Mexicans' backyard across the street and bring me a switch. You should find a good one from off them lemon trees."

"But, Momma, I can't. They have mean dogs back there. They'll get me."

"What, those little punk ass Rottweilers? Please, whatever goes down between you and those *ese vatos* is y'all's business. Geppetto told me to do this to help you. It's in your best interest to do what I say. *Capiche*? Be a man. Go get the switch." Her look told me she was sincere.

She not only beat me with a switch when I got punished, but she also did it with an extension cord, a shoe, and even her bare hands. I became numb after a while. One time, her choice of weapon was an iron. It was all because Geppetto said my mother should punish me for not taking out the trash.

"But I took out the garbage, Momma," I had said.

She had stood in front of me, trained as a hungry wolf. I was now the pig she was talking about. I imagined myself as a hog running through the woods until I found shelter inside an empty house. I yelled for Geppetto to let me in. "Open up! Wolf is coming!"

Momma was the big bad furry animal at the door, huffing and puffing and trying to blow her way in. "You think you're slick. But I saw you go in there. Either you come outside, or I'll blow this thing down."

I refused to come out. The wolf kept her promise and stormed her way in. I pictured sharp teeth plunging into my flesh like a stone thrown into a glass of water, ripping parts of me away until I escaped as a gut pile on the floor. The wolf chuckled and celebrated, looking at me like I was still there. She told me I tasted like "chicken."

I snapped back into reality.

"Dee. Do you hear me?" Momma had a weird look on her face. The vulnerability in her stare showed me how severe the confusion inside her was. "Geppetto's eyes are everywhere. He has no reason to lie. Telling the truth is that man's sin. Why do you want me to hurt you, Demetrius? Do you find joy in me bringing you pain?"

"No. I just don't want you to eat me."

"Eat you? Do you want to go to the farm?"

I shook my head. In her mind, the farm was real.

The farm was a world Geppetto created. She described it as a hidden place where he tortured children for misbehaving. It was in the most jaded part of her reality. Her mental illness never allowed her to envision the farm as being anything else other than what Geppetto told her. Nothing about it was make-believe.

"Geppetto can make it happen," she said. "There's a special place beneath the farm for bad kids like you. It's a world filled with fire. Everything that goes there burns for eternity. You want me to show you what that feels like?"

"No, ma'am."

"Yes, you do," she said.

"No, Momma. I believe you."

"No, you don't. Go to that closet and bring back that iron. Grab that extension cord, too."

I complied, even though it scared me. Terrified as a mouse, I had better reasons to cry. Walking down the hall, I saw pictures of the first eight years of my childhood watching me like obituaries with smiling faces. They all were laughing at me from both sides of the hallway. Every step I took was in sync with the funeral march inside me. Fate had my destiny sealed like a casket. The downside was there were no pallbearers to carry me. I had no choice but to walk as slow as death toward the Grim Reaper I called my mother.

"Hurry the fuck up. Momma needs to beat the molasses out of your ass. You're a little, slow-walking motherfucker."

As I headed into the living room where she was standing, she pulled a pack of Newport 100's from the pocket of her housecoat. "Smoking is bad," she said as she took out a cigarette and lit it. "You know, the white man invented smoking to kill minorities. Nicotine is like a roach spray for niggers. I better never catch you smoking. You understand me? Give me that iron! That extension cord, too."

I handed her both weapons.

"You stay put," she said.

So, like a statue, I didn't move. Momma headed over to an outlet on the wall and plugged in the iron. She made me wait until it got hot, then came back over with the red-heated steel. All I saw was the soleplate of that iron with a yellow spray button and black shell. It had a triangular shape that reminded me of a tombstone. The madness in her rose from the dead.

"Good things take time," she said. "Seeing good come from bad takes longer." She gestured, cueing me to come closer. "Come here, take off your shirt. It's time to burn you. Well, fuck it. Just get naked. Let's see that little dick," she said. "Decisions, decisions, decisions. Where do you want me to burn you?"

I didn't respond to the question.

"Answer me!" she said. "You want to look at me like you're crazy, huh? I said come here!" She used her free hand to grab my arm. She pulled me closer to her. The cigarette in her mouth had ashes over an inch long.

35

"Hold my cigarette," she said. "Don't let them ashes break."

There I was, naked, holding a cancer stick, moments from being burned by my mother. My nerves fell to the bottom of my feet. They were too afraid to travel up my spine. I needed God to be my savior and not allow fate to be a martyr. Fear poured out of my body until my anxiety was empty. Courage at that moment was best described as sacrificial: soft like a virgin, but brave as a lamb.

I had no choice.

"Take a deep breath. Show Momma your muscles. Inflate that chest," she said, touching the sculpted areas of my sleek upper torso. "Ooh, look at you, muscle man," she said. "You shouldn't be drinking milk. The doctor says you're lactose intolerant."

"I only drink milk at school."

"Shut up!" she said. "Talking too much makes it hard for me to burn you," she said, looking at my chest as if she was an artist looking to put a final touch on a painting. "Something's missing," she said. "I'll be right back. Hold this iron. Don't move." She handed me the iron to hold in my free hand. "Don't let those ashes fall." She headed toward the closet. "Let me find what else I need."

The iron wasn't too heavy. Still, it was clunky enough to challenge the arm that was free. Trying my best to hold the cigarette steady, I got nervous seeing

36

that burning orange ring and feeling the heat from the iron as I kept it above my waist, alongside my ribs. My bicep cramped and the cigarette ashes were a swat or two from breaking.

Momma came back from the closet with a spray bottle of starch and an ashtray.

"Give me that," she said, taking the cigarette from my hand, dumping the ashes, and placing it back into her mouth. "I have an idea," she said. She had a gift of talking and blowing at the same time. The cigarette would never leave her mouth. She kept the bottle of starch by her side. "Give me that iron, baby. Turn around in circles real slow for Momma."

I turned around in circles for her. That's when she sprayed me with the bottle of starch. The thick, slippery residue felt wet and sticky against my skin.

"See, this starch gonna allow me to iron you real good. When you get older, you'll thank me. Your skin will never have wrinkles."

As the steel plate of the iron came to within an inch of my chest, I took a step back. I guess that's when the temperature of my fear went cold; I shook, feeling the urge to urinate when my bladder released.

My mother saw the pee on the floor and stopped spraying. "Why you piss my floor, boy?"

"I had to go."

"Oh, you had to go. What a shame."

"Don't burn me, Momma."

She took one last puff of her cigarette, then put it out on the floor. She was still in front of me, holding the iron. "Anytime Momma hurts you, it's for your own good. You understand that, right?"

"No," I said.

She paused as if I'd pushed the right button. She glared into my soul. Maybe if I were a mirror that could have shown me as her, I would have better understood her reflection. I pictured the world inside her as an ecosphere of ice and frozen lakes. Anytime there was a warm emotion that came from her heart, the blood in her veins would turn to fire, causing all the ice in her world to melt away. Maybe that was the reason tears poured down her face like a river. Her body trembled. She moved closer. Her apologetic eyes were the same hazel as mine.

She lowered the iron and used her free hand to grab her favorite side of my face. It was the cheek that had a dimple. I could tell she was no longer going back and forth in her head. "I'll tell Geppetto Momma decided not to burn you. There's nothing in the world I wouldn't do for you. Thank God for allowing me to be your savior. Love you."

As she kissed me on the cheek, I saw the iron. "Love you, too, Momma." There was no other way I could respond.

Later that night, I received another visit from The Light.

# CHAPTER 8

# CHILD OF LIGHT

*Aunt Charlene*

When Olivia first came in contact with The Light, that child trembled something terrible. Confused. Speechless. Little Sister Girl wasn't able to identify what she'd seen—she'd turned nine the day before and hadn't feared dark since the start of her childhood years. But when The Light came, it was something different. It would appear and peel away from the blackness of a shadow as if it was a sticker pulled from a surface. Its brightness spiraled into this round orb that glowed with all these things that looked like shockwaves inside it; beautiful and perfect, it was as pretty as it was deadly. At the time, Olivia probably wasn't old enough to understand it or explain it to anybody, because The Light wasn't a ghost. Looking back, it was as if The Light was a magical living energy that had its own free will, and whoever held it inside was able to speak, and their face would show inside the ball. No one knew if it was good or evil, but it did once live in darkness. Pastor said, "Anything that comes from darkness can't be good." He taught that when God said, "Let there be Light," he made a mistake. His entire cult believed the same thing.

The moment Olivia came across it, The Light had a voice like an old man that sounded scary as the creaking of an old Victorian house with a cemetery next to it. The shadowy outlined face of a bearded man spilled out cracks of light as it appeared inside the floating orb.

"Hello, Olivia. You sure look pretty today," said the bearded face when it smiled.

"Thank you."

"Have you seen my daughter?"

"I don't know. Do she like dolls?"

"She sure does. She loves them almost as much as you."

"For real, because I have a lot of dolls. All of mine are black. My mother stopped buying me white girl dolls." Olivia thought, *Is this real?*

"Yes, my dearest child. This is very real," the voice said. The orb formed in the darkness. "What's wrong, did you never see The Light before?"

*How are you able to hear me in my head?*

"I'm The Light. I know all. I see all."

40

Other orbs eventually appeared and remained nearby.

"Do you trust me?"

"No."

"You will, darling," The Light said before fading away. "You will."

Olivia watched the bearded face in The Light.

CHAPTER 9

# 1 DIDN'T WANT HER TO LEAVE

The Light appeared once again as that ball of energy that floated over my bed, only this time it was a larger sphere filled with electricity. And it was no longer the size of a crystal ball. Its diameter was as big as the opening of a wastebasket. Its radiance glowed with a more intense brightness. It hovered above me as I lay beneath the covers, hoping to cry myself to sleep. It seemed the light had something it wanted to tell me. I usually would have been afraid, but this time I was too sad to be scared, although I was a tad nervous.

*What do you want?* I said in my head. Maybe it was there to console me. *Or to comfort me, not.*

"At least she didn't burn you. It could have been worse," The Light said. She spoke in the same young girl's voice I'd heard before. She was trying to comfort me.

"How do you know about that?" I asked, feeling both surprised and intrigued.

The same girl from before appeared as the shadowy face of The Light. "I know everything about you," she whispered.

"Everything? How do you know everything?" I said, feeling less and less nervous.

"Because I do," she said, sounding a bit snarky.

"No, you don't."

"I know everything about you, Demetrius."

"Well, enlighten me," I said, perking up a bit.

"Enlighten you? Did you say enlighten you? Wow! That's a mighty big word for someone who gets Cs in English."

"You know what I mean," I said, sitting up in bed. "Tell me something only I would know."

"Gladly," she said. "Tomorrow at school, a group of bullies will pick on you. One of them is a large older boy with funky teeth. If you want Natalie to like you, you need to stand up for yourself. Don't be afraid," she said as her face started disappearing slowly into the portal.

My fear must have taken a turn. I didn't want her to leave. "Wait! I need to know more," I said.

"Next time," she responded.

"Can you tell me your name? I thought you wanted to be my friend."

The Light didn't respond.

I tucked myself back under the covers, watching The Light vanish into the dark.

The next morning, I had school.

CHAPTER 10

# DOG FIGHT
# CENTRAL

James Baldwin Elementary was in a part of Hyde
Park, close to where they filmed the movie
*Boyz in the Hood*. When walking through the
neighborhood, I would think about the scene from
the movie where a group of young boys was walking
through an alley. One of them asks the others if they
want to see a dead body, so he shows them a cadaver
that has been lying around for days. The corpse is
that of a teenage boy, about seventeen, with a gunshot
wound to the chest. I often wondered how scared
Natalie would be if she saw a dead body.

Some mornings, we would take a shortcut up those
rusty out-of-service train tracks alongside Hyde Park
Boulevard. We would always see a dead dog or two. Their
corpses were always covered with bite marks around the

legs, throat, and neck. Some of them had parts of their ears and throats missing. They were usually leftovers from the night before.

A lot of drug dealers in our neighborhood gambled by betting on dogfights at the tracks. Most dogs lay in the alley for days after they died. The city was always slow picking them up. I wondered how slow they would be if those dogs were people.

Natalie hated walking through the alley. She never wanted to dirty up her Jordan high tops. Nats had on her favorite red number 23 Chicago Bulls Starter hoodie, basketball shorts, and yellow backpack, and thought she was dressed too fresh to be near the dumpsters in the alley. Natalie always complained, "Why do you even want to go this way, Dee? We need to find another route. This alley stinks." And she'd use her hand to cover her nose.

On this day, the alley smelled like rotting meat.

"We'll get to school faster this way," I said to her usual complaints. We had walked up on a couple of dead hounds. One of them was an albino pit bull with blood on its legs and abdomen, its entire throat missing—probably snatched by the other dog during the fight. Its mouth was stuck in a snarling grin that showed its sharp teeth.

I wanted Natalie to see it. "Look." I grabbed her arm to pull her closer to where I was. "You can tell she was ready to bite," I said.

46

"Don't try to make me stand close to that thing," Natalie said.

"Are you scared?"

"Are you?"

"No, but if she was alive, I would be. Let's check out the other dog," I said.

"You check it out. I'm staying right here," Natalie replied.

The other dog that had been in a fight with the pit bull was a large black Rottweiler that appeared not to have any injuries. Still, it looked dead. I wondered what caused it to die. "I don't see any blood or bite marks anywhere," I said, looking the dog over.

47

"Maybe it died lying on its wounds," Natalie said.

"Let's see."

"Oh, heck no, boy, you're crazy," Natalie said.

"No, I'm not. Go grab that stick for me," I said, pointing to an old broomstick lying against a nearby fence.

I had an idea to nudge the stick beneath the dog's stomach and flip it over onto its other side, which would have allowed us to see the wounds that it was lying on. I figured that the dog would have been stiff by now. After handing me the stick, Natalie reluctantly stood behind me. She seemed to know something unexpected was about to happen. I was studying the dog's dead body, trying to figure if nudging the stick beneath the side of its stomach would be the best approach.

I thought if I placed the stick underneath the side of its spine closest to the ground, I could flip it over without seeing its face.

"You sure it will work?" Natalie said.

"Yeah, I'm sure," I said.

"But don't you think that dog is too heavy to flip over? You're probably going to need another way to lift it."

*Good point!* I saw a "boulder-brick" sitting nearby. This was my nickname for chunky pieces of cement that broke off from either a wall or sidewalk and could be considered large rocks. The boulder-brick I spotted was a massive light gray chunk of broken cement from a nearby wall.

"Watch this," I said as I positioned the rock where I needed it to be. "This stick will go underneath the side of its stomach, and—*wham!* I'll tilt it against this rock like a seesaw and use all of my weight to flip it over."

"Be careful," Natalie said.

Too bad I didn't listen.

The outcome came out a lot different from what I had expected. As soon as I shoved the stick beneath the side of the dog, it sprung up on all fours, like it had come back to life or like one of those villains in a horror film that seem to be dead but were very much alive and just playing possum. This dog was also very much alive and now barking and growling. I knew it was too late to call on Jesus. Satan was already there to take the wheel. The dog's face looked like a demon had possessed it. The drool on its mouth was a thick, creamy white foam that reminded you of the froth on top of a cup of hot chocolate after all the marshmallows and whipped cream had melted. It was obviously mad. My reaction was to freeze because for a moment fear had taken away my instinct to run.

"Demetrius, don't move," Natalie said.

"I'm already on top of that," I replied.

"Good, stay put, cos I'm going to run." Natalie dashed down the alley full speed with her yellow bookbag dangling over her left shoulder.

*WOOF!* The dog took a step closer, snapping at me. I slowly took two steps back.

"Nice doggy," I said, watching Natalie's fleeing reflection in its reddish-brown eyes. Its growl became a deep gut rumble, like a chainsaw running out of gas. It shifted most of its weight onto its hind legs, like a canine version of a praying mantis, showing signs it was ready to spring into action, which would have most likely involved its teeth taking a bite out of somebody's ass.

I had two choices. Choice one was to save myself— run as fast as I could up the alley until I could hop a fence into somebody's backyard. Choice two was to save Natalie by distracting the dog and forcing it to chase me. Since I knew I was a faster runner than she was, I figured that was the best choice.

"Keep running, Natalie!" I shouted.

I swung my stick at the dog's horrid face, aiming for its nose. Its reflexes were incredible: it caught the stick and held it with its front teeth, locking down on the wood using the sharp premolars on the top and bottom of its thick, muscular jaws. It pulled me its way. I heaved back in the opposite direction, forcing the dog to tug against me.

As he yanked the stick harder, I let it go, knowing he'd be off balance due to the force of its own strength, and I would gain a few seconds before he would be able to bite me, because he would take at least a second to drop the stick.

I only needed about a three-second head start. By then, Natalie would have had an even better head start and a separate route to get away. As the dog tried to regain its balance, I sprinted up the alley as fast as I could. Running made me feel closer to safety. I saw Natalie had made it clear to the opening onto the next block.

The dog chased me, but I hopped a fence too high for the dog to get over. I cut through someone's backyard and headed through the neighborhood, making my way to school. On residential blocks, Hyde Park had a lot of small homes with iron doors and lawns surrounded by metal fences. Some windows had posted signs with a picture of a man holding a gun that said "Beware of Owner," which made me feel like I would get shot.

Other signs said "Neighborhood Watch," and those made me feel like I was being spied on. The only thing good about my apartment was that there were no signs in the windows. The yards with the most beautiful houses had chained up their vicious dogs that barked when I walked past.

I didn't see Natalie, so I headed off to school.

# CHAPTER 11

# KUNG FU CRACK BABY

Older kids at school called me "Kung Fu Crack Baby" because my mother took drugs and my favorite kicks were a pair of holey karate shoes two sizes too big. The best part of my wardrobe was a black Member's Only jacket that smelled like Old Spice, cigarettes, and cocoa butter that Momma bought from the secondhand store. A day never went by without me getting clowned for wearing hand-me-down clothes. I was a nerd because I was into karate movies and pro-wrestling. Hulk Hogan and Randy "Macho Man" Savage were my favorite wrestling superstars. Hulk never backed down from an opponent, no matter how big they were, while Macho Man always screamed cool things to the audience.

I was also into karate movies. My favorites were *The Last Dragon, The Karate Kid,* and any film that starred Bruce Lee. He was a badass and made funny noises when he fought. *The Last Dragon* was the story of Leroy Green, a kid in the ghetto who trained to attain the same level of mastery as the great Bruce Lee, *my hero.* One night, Leroy's life changed forever. He rescues a famous television personality named Laura Charles from the evil mob leader, Eddie Arkadian, saving her life. Laura starts to like Leroy and gives him a juicy kiss at the end of the movie, which made being a kung fu hero look cool. Natalie was my Laura Charles. *The Karate Kid* is about a teenager named Daniel who gets bullied until he stands up and fights for himself. Leroy and Daniel were like me—social outcasts who didn't have friends. I aspired to be like them and the heroes I looked up to. It was the only way I could get through school.

I had a hard time outside class. Teachers were never around when I was being bullied. But with The Light in my corner, I could make that all change. That day would be the moment when I finally became the victor.

I arrived at school, which was an off-white graffiti spectacle of a building that looked like it was a semester or two from dying of old age. Walking down the halls made me feel I'd been swallowed alive, passing down into the belly of a fire-breathing dragon until I was defecated into my fourth-grade classroom that smelled like urine. I hated going to school. I had reading and math that morning.

When it was time for lunch, I followed the smell of chocolate milk and welfare burgers to the cafeteria. Tommy and his crew of older bullies pushed their way through the line where I was standing. They were shouting and surrounded me.

"Leave me alone," I said. I intended to let Tommy and his boys know I meant business.

Big Boy Tommy pushed me to the ground. "Get out of my line! Skinny punk!"

54

I scraped my elbow during the fall. "Ow!" I said, looking at the drippy liquid redness thickening in the creases of my dark skin. Tommy and his goons laughed at my bleeding elbow.

"Why you do that?" I said, trying my best to fight back my hurt, but my voice trembled with pain.

"Because I can," he said.

Tommy bullied me every day because he knew I was too small to fight back, but every dog has his day. If he wasn't pranking me and calling me names, he was punching me or pushing me to the ground whenever he saw me. The Light had told me I needed to stand up for myself, and the time was now. Enough was enough; I was tired of being picked on and it was going to be the last time that a bully ever pushed me to the ground and made fun of me. I knew that day would be the day things changed.

I was a small nine-year-old who didn't care if that jiggly Dumbo-eared bastard with a lazy eye and buckteeth was a fifth-grader. I was half his size, had never fought before, and couldn't bust a grape in a fruit fight, but I had fantasies about kicking his ass.

One fantasy was a wrestling match between Tommy and me identical to the war between Hulk Hogan and Andre the Giant, where I played the Hulkster, and Big Ears was more like the fat fellow. In the original match, Hogan stood up to Andre, even though the Giant was much bigger and stronger and at one point beat up his smaller opponent. Hulk held his ground, picked up the Giant, and slammed him to the mat, pinning and defeating him. In the bout that happened in my head, I did the same thing as Hogan, except I did it faster and better, and then ring girls kissed me on the cheek and said they loved me, and the audience cheered and chanted my name.

Tommy would get up off the mat and sneak up behind me while the ladies and roaring crowd still adored me. The women thought I was so suave. I would be smoother than LL Cool J in his *I Need Love* music video, minus his muscles, gold chain, moist lips, and Kangol hat. As one of the ring girls wiped their lipstick from my cheek, Fat Boy got closer. I sensed it, moved the ladies out of the way, and flung him against the ropes. He bounced off them and ran back toward me. I threw him into a turnbuckle, came over to him, and unloaded several elbows to his frontal lobe and kisser.

The crowd yelled, "Finish him!"

Dazed, Fat Boo-Boo Boy Tommy stumbled out into the center of the fight circle.

It was the perfect time to deliver that front kick to his face. He fell to the mat, belly up, with a bleeding forehead in all its gore and glory. Spectators egged me on. They wanted me to perform a bigger and better move. They continually shouted, "Leg, drop!" I obliged by leaping upward, hoisting and kicking out my leg while in midair, and tightening my quadriceps with as much pressure as I possibly could.

A split second later, I came down hard on his throat with the rear of my calf. *BAM!* I finished Tommy with one of Hogan's signature moves. I stood in the ring, celebrating and posing for the fans. I even had a slogan where I said, "Whatcha gonna do when Demetrius Daredevil runs wild on you!"

In the real world, the fight was different. After Tommy pushed me to the ground, I got up and stood on my feet, wiping off the burger, fries, and salad that came from the lunch tray. I thought of The Light and what it told me to do.

"I'm tired of you picking on me, Fat Boy!" I shouted.

"Don't call me fat, you little nappy-headed motherfucker! I'm not fat. I'm big-boned."

"Yeah, your bones are big, just like your ass!" I yelled.

Everyone laughed, even a few members of his crew. Tommy pointed at my feet. "Get out of here with those holey karate shoes."

"There's nothing wrong with my shoes," I said.

"Fool please, those shoes are the only shoes your momma can afford because that bitch is a crackhead. And you're nothing but a little crack baby."

"Forget you, Fat Boy. You don't know nothing about my momma!"

Tommy got more in my face. By now, all the kids in the lunchroom had formed a circle around us. We were the main attraction. Natalie was there, looking concerned and worried I was going to get crushed. Tommy continued ragging on me.

"I know your momma is on crack because my daddy is the dope man who sells it to her! I always see her walk up to him on the corner and give him money. Then she walks away with the stuff he hands her. I know she goes home and smokes it. She probably smokes it with your bony ass, crack boy!"

"You don't even know what you're talking about, stupid. You're a liar! You ever look to see what's in her hand?"

"What makes me a liar? Crack baby!"

"Because my momma is not on crack. She's on heroin!" I said.

The entire lunchroom erupted in laughter.

Tommy stood in front of me, dumbfounded. I couldn't tell if he wanted to laugh or hit me, but either way, I was prepared. Not only as a wrestling fan but also as a connoisseur of martial arts movies who would practice karate in his head, I had the perfect move saved for someone like Tommy.

The move was a kicking technique called "The Butterfly" that I saw in the film *The Karate Kid*, where the main character Daniel did a pose, balancing himself on one foot with both of his arms to the side, moments before performing a targeted kick to his opponent's face, bringing him down. I knew if Tommy attacked me, I could make that move happen. I got in my stance.

"Prepare to die!" I said. Tommy had his warning.

Even though I was mimicking a fight move from *The Karate Kid*, everything I said sounded like something Bruce Lee would say in a movie. I guess I'd been watching too much Kung Fu Theater. I spoke with an Asian accent, trying my best to sound like a character from an English-dubbed film.

"My body is a lethal weapon, my fat, fine, fluffy friend. Any enemy that attacks me will succumb to a terrible defeat and die. I am the grandest of all grandmasters. I must warn you. My martial art is my war. If you come any closer, you will experience the wrath of my butterfly. This technique is as beautiful as it is deadly. You'll die a thousand deaths," I said, sounding weird as cat shit.

Tommy looked at me and said, "This nigga's crazy."

"No one's crazy, Fat Boy. I'm just one with the wind," I said.

Focused and more comfortable in my pose, I took a deep breath and exhaled. If the fight that was about to happen were a scene in a karate movie, this would be the part of the film where I started glowing like Bruce Leroy from *Last Dragon*. I was ready to strike.

"Come get this whopping! My foot must become one with your behind."

Ole fatty fat moved in quickly to pounce. Still in my stance, I executed the kick, except I didn't hit my target.  Instead, my shoe flew off and hit the school principal as he walked toward us. I was immediately angry at The Light for encouraging me to do such a dumb thing.

As Tommy and I were hauled away to the principal's office, he looked over at me and uttered the words, "I hate you."

I told him, "I hate you, too."

CHAPTER 12

# FREEDOM FIGHTERS AND CATERPILLARS

After our fight, Tommy and I ended up in the principal's office. The office was spacious with a cherry wood mahogany desk topped with shiny gold pens, matching leather chairs, and plush dark brown carpet that sprung back when someone walked across it. The office was the only room in the school with an air conditioner that worked. On hot days, kids got in trouble on purpose just to come to the office for cool air. The principal also had an exotic goldfish that seemed out of place in an aquarium full of seahorses.

Tommy and I sat a couple of seats away from each other in front of the principal's desk. Tommy reminded me of those bullies from those Saturday afternoon specials about bigger kids who picked on smaller children because of their terrible lives at home. The principal, Dr. Sherrod Jackson, reminded me of all the things I hated watching on television: He looked like the black guy who wore the purple grape costume in those *Fruit of the Loom* commercials.

His thick West Indian accent reminded me of those men on the Royal Caribbean boat advertisements that played between my two favorite cartoons, *Teenage Mutant Ninja Turtles* and *Bionic Six*. And the boring suits he wore reminded me of token black guys on those predominantly white sitcoms I could never sit through, like Isaac Washington on *The Love Boat*.

I really hated his lectures. Now and then, when Dr. Sherrod Jackson wasn't paying attention, Tommy would give me the middle finger. I would respond by sticking out my tongue, and then Dr. Jackson would tell us to "cut it out" and "behave." Neither one of us was listening. "Neither one of you has an excuse to involve yourselves in a fight" was probably Dr. Jackson's logical response to our fight. "But he started it" is something Tommy would have said.

Dr. Jackson would have responded by telling him to "be quiet." And he probably said, "How would you feel if someone picked on you, Thomas?" or "You could have just walked away, Demetrius." I can't remember what I told him about how the fight got started.

At some point, he asked Tommy to step out of his office into the waiting area so he could talk to me alone.

He told Tommy to "sit on that chair and stay put" and he complied, dragging his feet. "Whatever, man," Tommy said, shutting the door.

Dr. Jackson had a white wife. She was the younger blonde with dreadlocks in the photos on the wall. Her pictures were next to numerous black and white photographs featuring historical moments of the civil rights movement.

Even at nine years old, I knew there was no such thing as love in the African-American community. All the positive black male role models disappeared during the civil rights era, which was twenty-five years before my time, and that was exactly what those old pictures on the wall reminded me of: a bunch of dead black men who were no longer around to fight for the black struggle. I guess Dr. Jackson was doing the best that he could with us black boys in the inner city.

He got up from out of his seat and headed over to the wall. "Demetrius, my young boy, you disappointed me today. Whenever you disappoint me, sir, you disappoint them," he said, pointing to the wall. "Do you know who these people are?" he asked.

*Yes, they are freedom fighters,* I said to myself, but I shook my head no. I wanted him to think he was telling me something new. Although I had heard this speech many times, he never seemed to remember.

"Those men and women are what you call freedom fighters. They are the ones who fought for your freedom," he said. "When I say freedom, Demetrius, what type of freedom am I referring to, sir?"

"When you say freedom, you are not only talking about freedom for black people, but for all people," I responded.

"Yes, all people. So, when you disappoint them, you become a dissatisfaction to everyone, my son, including yourself," Dr. Jackson said, taking a seat on the corner edge of his desk.

"What do you mean?" I said aloud. "How can I disappoint myself?" I asked, even though I knew his answer.

"You disappoint yourself by not living up to your full potential. Are you familiar with caterpillars, Demetrius?"

"Yes, a little. Why?"

"I want you think of yourself as a social caterpillar that is afraid to blossom. But with enough light shone on your strong African spirit, you will become a butterfly with beautiful, colorful wings, my boy, "Dr. Jackson said, picking up a replica of a butterfly sitting on his desk, twirling it around in his hand. "Wings you can grow if you choose to learn how to blossom." Dr. Jackson said, pointing the butterfly at me. "If you do, you'll be able to soar in the sky with the strength of an eagle. All you have to do is stay focused and not allow your surroundings to overcome you. This is something you can do, Demetrius, I believe you will have a strong future as a positive black man." He placed the butterfly back on his desk.

*But I don't believe in you,* I said in my head, taking a deep breath, thinking about all the insanity that had happened that day.

I eventually ended up heading to class in time for my social studies period.

# CHAPTER 13

# I WAS CURIOUS ABOUT HER LAUGHTER

I returned home from school, hoping I could make it to my room before being confronted by my mother about the fight I had during lunch. From the front door, I saw her asleep on the couch wearing her favorite yellow housecoat that reminded me of a traffic light.

I made no noise as I tiptoed across the living room. Momma was a heavy sleeper, and she was fast asleep when I stepped into the hallway near my bedroom, but her voice came out of nowhere.

"Demetrius," she said. The way she spoke made me stop dead in my tracks.

"Yes, Momma." My voice trembled as I froze and thawed simultaneously, feeling the moisture of warm sweat slither like a snake down my spine. I turned around and saw her still on the couch, her eyes closed.

"I heard about that fight you had at school," she said.

"But I wasn't the one who started it," I said.

"Geppetto thinks differently. He's going to get you good, and there's nothing I can do to tell him not to," she said.

I didn't respond and instead headed to my room. It would not be the first time Geppetto punished me.

Later that night, as I was finishing my homework, the entire room turned pitch black. I assumed the electricity went out until I heard a child's giggle coming from my bedroom closet. Bright white light poured from underneath the closet door. I smelled jasmine and orange candy, the same aroma I sensed anytime I got a visit from The Light. But I knew it was something different this time.

I got up from off the floor and slowly headed toward the closet door. A part of me was nervous, yet another part of me knew I had to overcome my fear. Anxiety had been my biggest burden. Being afraid to be brave had been an obstacle my entire life, and this was similar.

"Hello," I said. I was only a couple of steps away from opening the closet. "Is anyone there?" I had hoped to get an answer, but unfortunately got no response, only giggles. The Light had something up its sleeve. "What do you want?" I said.

"Whatever you want," said The Light. It sounded like the girl that had shown her face to me.

I didn't want to see her again. I was mad at her for encouraging me to stand up to Tommy and getting me into a fight. By this time, I was standing in front of the closet door, pondering whether I should open it up. *Should I?* I said in my head. Without thinking, I opened the door and saw a translucent, glowing body of light with a large shadowy image of someone inside it. Their body swayed back and forth. Something about the way they moved made me want to get closer. As I attempted to walk through the portal to get to the other side, I got stuck inside a rubbery, gum-like surface that prevented me from breaking through its wall. I used the weight of my body to push as hard as I could.

"Push! Break through the layer," The Light said. "Find me if you can. The game is called hide-and-go-seek. Remember?"

I broke through the layer, and there it was: a new world filled with life from a different time.

Everything around me proved I was no longer in 1992. I stood in the living room of a small country home with a chimney, old floors, and a tin roof—a picture of Franklin Roosevelt was on a nearby wall. The house smelled like the warmth from burning wood, baked bread, bacon, and brewed coffee. I hadn't eaten lunch at school, so thinking about food was torture. My stomach growled. I placed a hand over my belly. *Hang in there*, I said silently. *Bang!* I heard a slam, and static fizzled out behind me. When I turned around, I saw the portal had gone. My chances of returning home were now impossible. The orange hue from the fireplace illuminated a shadow on the wall of a large, elderly, heavy-set Caucasian woman, who swayed back and forth in her rocking chair, knitting a green blanket. I tried to hide behind a nearby sofa, hoping she wouldn't see me, but she did.

"Where do you think you are going, blackie?" she said in a thick Irish accent. "Do you think me wits have gone away? You think I would not detect a sneaky moon cricket hopping away in me home, did you? I should put some leather to your backside, I say. You can come out of hiding now," she said, eyeing me over her glasses.

I came out of hiding and headed over to where she was in the rocking chair. Next to her was a large tin can full of spit that came from her chewing tobacco.

"Know who I am?" she said.

"No."

"I'm your great-great-grandmother, me boy. You can call me Grandma Cindy," she replied.

"But you're white," I said.

"Yeah, and you're a little blackie, but it's not your fault."

She spat spit from her chewing tobacco in my eye, and then everything went black.

The next morning, I woke in my bed. I figured it was some crazy dream until I noticed the green blanket covering me, which Grandma Cindy said she was knitting for me.

# CHAPTER 14

# I DIDN'T RESPECT HIM

R egardless of how bad Geppetto treated me, she told me I still had to respect him. You see, she claimed Geppetto saved my life at birth.

Nine months after her thirteenth birthday, my mother conceived me. By the time she was fourteen, her belly was showing, and after 273 days of pregnancy, the 274th day must have been the most important day of them all, since it marked the day she went into labor with me. Momma told me Geppetto opened a magical iron door attached to the internal wall of her belly. She said the door he opened was not only my re-entry into a new life, but it was also an exit from a dimly lit world filled with spirits waiting to become human again.

She taught me that babies didn't really come from mommies but a secret layer of heaven hidden in darkness. It was the same place where the moon hid from the world when the sun came out. She told me the place was called Satan. Satan was not a fallen angel from heaven named Lucifer, but a sacred layer of darkness where farms were filled with fields of closed caskets sitting on top of graves. Within every casket, seeds sprouted into lifeless babies waiting to be born. Each coffin held a seed until it was an unborn corpse. Every corpse, of course, was the dead body of an infant. Like a clam opening onto a pearl, a coffin opened every time a new seed sprouted. New crops came every full moon. The moon would shine a light on every coffin until each seed grew into a corpse. Once the dead body appeared, a soul would enter through its mouth, causing the child's heart to beat. My mother said the moon was the reason children were born.

"So, is the moon my daddy?" I asked.

"No!" she replied.

"Why not?" I said.

"Because, the moon doesn't have a dick."

Regardless if it was day or night, Geppetto would get a signal in the sky telling him how to find the woman that was expected to deliver. He would arrive moments before she went into labor. If there were mommies in the world giving birth at the same time, Geppetto could be in more than one place. Every time Geppetto opened the door to pull a child out of a woman's womb, he would ask her if she wanted a boy or girl. He'd ask if she wanted twins, or even triplets, or sometimes more children than a woman could count on her fingers.

So, Geppetto would reach in and pull you from out of the darkness into a world filled with light. Before you were named, he'd spank your behind so you could catch enough air. Geppetto would cut the umbilical cord as soon as a child was pulled from out of the mother. The umbilical cord was a root that sprouted from the seed the child came from. That root was the last connection to the farm inside the woman. During pregnancy, sharecroppers used the root as a source of delivering nutrients to an unborn child once its heart started beating. If the root wasn't cut as soon as the child was born, the farmers used the cord to yank the child out of Geppetto's arms. The infant would then go back to the farm inside the mother's womb. There, it slowly turned back into a corpse and would begin to rot like an overripe fruit. Once maggots started eating the body, an open coffin would emerge from the dirt beneath it, and then slam its lid like an alligator trapping its prey. When the body was completely inside its interior, the casket would slowly sink into the ground like an animal stuck in quicksand. Geppetto's job was to make sure that type of thing never happened.

But when I was born, I couldn't breathe. Geppetto smacked me on the backside, so I would cry and suck in the fresh air. Momma said not being able to breathe at birth was like being born dead with a heartbeat.

Momma said birth and death were sort of the same thing; death was life waiting to be unborn.

Geppetto saved me from death. It was his responsibility to name every child in the world. So, in 1983, Geppetto named me Demetrius, along with six thousand other kids. I never understood why an Italian man would give a black boy a Greek name. Momma said my name had two different meanings. In something that white people called Greek mythology, it meant "lover of the Earth." The other meaning came from the Bible and meant upholder of the truth. My mother said  that when Geppetto first looked in my eyes, he could tell I would go through life without ever telling a lie.

CHAPTER 15

# NOT THE SON HE NEVER HAD

73

One thing Geppetto had in common with my father is that they both were invisible men. I never saw them. Even if mom was better at keeping Dad away, I still had a parent who didn't hit me. Our building stayed mostly filled with struggling mothers like mine, who never understood what it meant to catch a break. If life was a fight to live sober, most of the women in Park Arms were casualties of the drug war.

They never were successful in fighting off the demons that caused people to get high. A good number of them sold sex to catch that feeling. From sunup to sundown, they roamed the streets like animals searching for food. Their addiction is what needed to be fed.

Momma referred to her drugs as "candy." Probably because of how they made her feel, or maybe because of the way they tasted. Her sugar daddies kept her from roaming the streets when Geppetto wasn't around. She told me Geppetto never wanted her to go out. He felt it was best for her safety; Geppetto didn't want her harmed or touched by another person. He wanted to be the one leaving the bruises.

But there were nights when she scratched the itch to get out the house. She'd tell me Geppetto was in her room in case something happened. I'd tell her it wasn't necessary for him to be there. I was big enough to babysit myself.

"Make like a trap and shut your mouth!" she'd say. "Get like a truck and park yourself. Be like a seed and plant your ass on that couch!" If I didn't, she threatened and told me, "I'll fuck you up!" Inside my head, I was like, *Whatever!* I didn't need Geppetto telling me what to do. He had never met me. He had never come out of that stank bedroom one time to say "hello." I never even saw him arrive, although I had prayed to see him leave. To simply glimpse him walking out the door, I would have done anything my mother said for the rest of my life.

I would spend hours searching her room for Geppetto. I could never track him down. He must have had a secret way to get in or out of her room without me knowing. He must've been hiding inside her belly. The farm inside of her had a lot of dark places he could duck behind.

Any time my mother went out, I wouldn't watch TV, nor would I go to sleep. I would stay on the couch with my eyes and ears zoned in on her bedroom door, listening out for any sounds that came from behind it. Geppetto was so quiet. He had the gift of being silent. I was up until she came home. When my mother got in, she would either be drunk or high, or sometimes both. Never sober enough to tuck me into bed, nor happy enough to give me a hug.

One night, when I was around seven years old, I was up on the couch waiting for Momma when she staggered through the door, wearing a black baby doll dress and matching leather boots. She pointed to my room and said, "That way! You better be careful counting those sheep. If you don't cover up when you see them hopping over your head, they'll shit and piss all over your face. You need to sleep with your umbrella up."

"I don't have an umbrella," I said while walking toward my room in my Batman pajamas.

"Suit yourself. I ain't cleaning up nothing!"

"Don't worry, Mom. I'll be okay."

"How's that?" she said.

I turned around to get a last look at her before I went into my room. She was standing in the living room with a hand on her hip. "I'll be sure to count sheep backwards, Momma. So, if they pee or poo, they'll take it with them when they hop over my head. You know, sort of like a VCR when you press the rewind button."

"Damn, nigga knowledge! Good night to you, too."

"Mom, it's 6 a.m. Good morning."

"Carry your ass to bed!"

I went into my room and closed the door, but I didn't go to sleep. I wanted to know if something was going to happen between her and Geppetto. So, I waited for a few moments before sneaking out of my room. In the hall, outside of her bedroom, I heard my mom giving Geppetto a piece of her twisted mind. I imagined Geppetto confronting her about coming home in the wee hours of the morning. She knew she had a son to take care of, but frankly, she was behaving like a bad mother. I pressed an ear against the wall to get a better listen.

"There is no other place a bitch belongs besides here with your big, numb, dumb, hokey pokey joke of a broke ass," she said. "Always fussing like an old woman and shit. I came back for you, you ungrateful, mediocre, mile-a-minute, Geritol-popping motherfucker. Me and my son could have left together, forever! Mama bird and baby bird don't need wings to fly. We could have caught an airplane. Don't get it twisted. Trusting you around him is me trusting you. Thou shall not be a goddamn, punk ass, godforsaken liar! Hell shall have no mercy on a mark ass, buster ass, bitch ass nigga who chooses otherwise. Yeah, I know you ain't black, but Negroes don't have color around this house. Do you feel me?!" she said, after ending every sentence with an underlying conviction that could have prosecuted an angel. There was a pause in her banter, as if God had taken the battery out of her back. A moment went by before I heard her voice lower to a raspy whisper, choking on the words, "I just want you to trust me." Her voice cracked as if she was about to cry. "Do you trust me, Geppetto?"

During nights where my mother fussed at Geppetto, her silence ceased after the sounds of shattered glass and her falling against the floor. I'd check on her by banging on the locked door to her room.

"Momma, are you okay? Answer me!"

She would never respond, but her heavy snores told me she was okay. Her snores kept me from calling the police.

The next morning, she would enter the living room, looking like she had been in a fight. She would put an ice pack on her sores and swellings, and had several ways to cover up the discoloration to her face and arms.

She would tell me the story of Geppetto. He was once a puppeteer in Italy who couldn't have children. She said someone told her he even referred to one of his wooden puppets as the son he never had. The puppet ended his life, wanting to become a real boy.

# CHAPTER 16

# COTTON BALLS IN THE SKY

I was lying under the covers, waiting to fall asleep when it came. The Light was a sight I didn't want to see. It moved across the room faster than usual. I didn't want any part of what it had to offer.

"Go away!" I said. "I don't want you here!"

The Light refused to leave, flying around in circles until it stopped to hover over me. It bounced in place like it was anxious, speaking in the voice of that girl.

"I don't want to go away," she said.

"I don't want to play any more games," I said.

"I'm not here to play a game, Demetrius."

"Why did you make me go in that portal with that big white lady?"

"That lady was your great-great-grandmother."

"She called me blackie. I don't like her," I said.

"She's not as mean as you think. You have to give her a chance to grow on you."

"She sure could have fooled me. If she's my great-great-granny, why has no one ever told me who she is? And why's she white, and Irish?"

"And what happened after the chicken crossed the road?" The Light responded.

"I don't know," I replied, shrugging my shoulders. I was still beneath the covers. "Anyway, how would you know if she was my granny?"

"The Light knows everything."

"Everything?"

"Yes, everything," The Light said, still bouncing in place. "Do you want to hear a story?"

"No, stories are boring," I answered.

"Not this one," The Light said. "Let me show you."

The Light vanished, and the room went from dark to pitch black, from white noise to total silence. I held on tightly to the covers, hiding underneath them. And that's when the ceiling transformed into a hovering plane of light with rippling waves of blue energy inside it. The waves of energy first started at the center of the ceiling before spreading out like electric tentacles to the corners, and then down the dark walls at the edges of its surrounding angles, until the entire room became a box of light. The floor beneath me was the last part of my bedroom that remained, and then, soon enough, it had gone away.

Scenes from my great-great-granny's life played at lightning speed on the wall that was once a ceiling above me. I saw everything—from the time she was born until her passing as an elderly woman, and then back to her life as a kid on a farm. The last thing I saw on the wall was an image of an empty potato field, and then there was another flash of light.

I woke up in a strange place. I was lying on my back, in the middle of an empty potato field. All I had on was white Scooby-Doo underwear I wished I hadn't worn. The clouds above me were huge, puffy cotton balls that moved slowly like icebergs in the ocean. All these weirdly shaped potatoes next to me looked like big brown rocks that hid under small dying plants with black withered leaves that swayed back and forth in the wind. Potato plants laid in lazy rows across the field. I hoped I wouldn't be here too long. I hated potatoes.

The air was as cold and wet as a glass of ice water. I began trembling. I folded my arms across my chest and rubbed my hands up and down my sides, hugging myself to keep warm. The smell of that soft, damp, itchy mixture of soil and seabird guano must have intoxicated those goosebumps that crawled onto all the places I had skin. I felt them tingling up in the crevices of those inappropriate places that I prefer not to mention, if you know what I mean.

I got up from the ground and attempted to wipe off the crud I had on me. I looked around. On the other side of the field was a white girl who looked close to my age. She had appeared out of nowhere, dressed like a pilgrim. She wore a long, black farm dress with a white apron and black lace-up boots. On her head, she wore a white bonnet that matched the shawl around her neck. Her cheeks were as rosy and red as the curls in her hair, and her eyes were as green as pastures. I wanted her attention. I thought she could help me figure out where I was.

"Hello!" I said, once again hugging myself to keep warm. "Can you tell me where I am?"

She didn't respond and took a couple of steps around the field's edge to avoid walking toward me or stepping in the dirt. Then she held out her arm. She was holding something in her hand. The way she held it let me know she wanted me to have it.

Once I walked over, I saw what was in her hand—a glowing potato.

"Take it. This is yours," she said in a thick Irish accent. "They're not that great to eat."

I stared at the potato, wondering why she handed it to me and what was making it glow. I held it in one hand as I slowly slid the tip of my index finger vertically down the center. The potato suddenly split in two halves. Inside the potato were soft dark spots that felt really gooey. They felt like warm chocolate chips. The potato stunk badly. It smelled worse than those dead dogs Natalie and I had found in the alley. I covered my nose, feeling nauseous. There was a flash of light.

I woke up in my bed in a cold sweat. On top of my lap, above the covers, I saw the split potato. I picked up both halves to confirm it was real, and then the smell hit me. I became nauseous again, threw the potato on the floor, and used my left hand to toss off the covers. I placed my right hand over my mouth to stop myself from puking, and I ran out of my bedroom to the toilet to throw up. The puke was chunky and yellow and tasted like it had been sitting in my stomach for days.

When I went back to my room, the potato was still there. It took a lot more visits from The Light to learn about the story of the glowing potato.

CHAPTER 17

# TORNADOS, GHETTO BIRDS, AND MAGICAL HOOD WITCHES

S cience was my favorite subject in school, especially when Mr. Hughley taught it. He was a scientist at NASA who became inspired to teach kids about science, math, and technology after seeing the movie *Lean on Me*. While going to class made me think about movies, TV shows, and comic books, Mr. Hughley, for the most part, made me think about motion pictures.

*Lean on Me* was the film where Morgan Freeman played a character named Joe Clark, who everyone called "Crazy Joe." Joe became a principal at a high school that had a bunch of failing students. My favorite character in that movie was a fat kid named Thomas

Sams. Thomas was a good kid who always got into trouble. Even though I wasn't overweight, I pictured myself as fat Sams and Mr. Hughley as Joe Clark. Although Hughley was a lot nicer than Clark and Sams was a good kid that kept getting into trouble, I rarely got into many mishaps, except for that one thing with Tommy, but you know that story (my fantasy about kicking his ass turned into a nightmare).

Anyway, I always imagined Hughley daring me to jump off the roof of the school's main building, just as Joe told Sams to do in the movie. Except, I would  actually do it. Hughley would be surprised when I jumped off the roof because I would never hit the ground, thanks to the rocket booster beneath my backpack that launched me upward into the sky. I would then fly around the campus, and the kids would watch. Hughley would laugh and be amazed I'd made my own rocket. I would get an A at the end of the semester. For us inner-city kids, learning about something other than the typical math, reading, and science lessons was vital. Plus, it was even more imperative for everyone to know that there was a world outside the bubble we lived in. Mr. Hughley provided that, because to him Hyde Park wasn't just the hood; it was where he grew up.

He was a short, stout, four-eyed, bald, dark brother who had a head shaved so clean it reminded you of a Hershey's Milk Dud or one of those chocolate M&M's. I swore that if anyone got close enough to his cranium, they would see their reflection in Mr. Hughley's big ole shiny head. He called us all his little scientists and made us put on lab coats like the one he always wore every time he came to class.

He had a deep booming voice and always got excited when the things he brought in for us to check out intrigued us; like the one time when he brought in this big piece of dinged up metal that had burn marks around the edges. I was curious about what it was, so I raised my hand in class to find out more about it.

"Mr. Hughley. What is that?!"

"It's a piece of a rocket ship, Demetrius."

"From outer space?"

"Yes."

"Whoa!"

"Do you want to touch it?"

"Oh, fo' sho, Big Homey."

"You mean 'for sure,' Demetrius. I am not your homey."

"Sorry. I mean for sure, Mr. Hughley."

"Well, so be it. Class, gather around."

When I got my chance to touch the metal, I was surprised how cold it was; I initially imagined it being hot since it came from outer space and all. The rockets I saw on television were launched into the sky, shedding off parts of their shell while soaring at fast speeds out of the Earth's atmosphere. I remembered when Mr. Hughley taught us about thermal rockets and how they were heated by nuclear power, which would make the metal from the shuttle extremely hot. Then I started thinking about movies. I wondered if the metal on all those spaceships in those *Star Wars* and *Star Trek* movies felt as cool as the piece of rocket ship Hughley brought to class. I never saw Han Solo or Luke Skywalker touch the outside of their spaceship, so I never had an assumption about the temperature of anything that orbited around the solar system without being attacked by aliens. If Dr. Spock had touched anywhere on the outer part of the USS Enterprise that was extremely hot, he would have used his Vulcan powers to lower the temperature.

One time Hughley brought in a storm machine and made a tornado happen in class. It reminded me of a scene from *The Wizard of Oz*. You know, that scene where Dorothy gets trapped in a windstorm and she and her dog Toto are both swept away in a twister— she looks out the window and sees different people floating past her house in the sky. I watched the tornado Hughley created, which even sucked a toy cow off the farm replica he had put together for his presentation. My mouth stayed agape seeing that plastic cow twirl around in Hughley's whirlwind.

I imagined Dorothy was afraid when she saw that witch flying by her window. Mr. Hughley continued with his presentation, and I looked out the window to see what was happening, and there I saw it. A big black "ghetto bird" hovering over the school, like a hawk eyeing its prey. Its head was four swirling, chopping blades that continuously cut the wind, and its eyes two white men in black uniforms behind two glass windows. I couldn't take my eyes off the large white letters and numbers I saw underneath its belly. It was a monster in the big blue yonder zeroing in on the open field nearest to my classroom. Although many had tried, there was no way to kill a ghetto bird. Those things stayed flying in the sky.

A ghetto bird was a police helicopter that flew around black neighborhoods in search of crime and people who ran from police. A few kids in class said the ghetto bird was looking for the "Hood Witch," who was on the run for killing a bunch of bad cops.

The Hood Witch was allegedly a magical spirit lady that lived inside the abandoned dope house where her son was murdered. After his death, she had a nervous breakdown and returned as a vigilante around Crenshaw. The Hood Witch protected people from bad cops and gangs, and healed the sick. Even though I'd never seen her, she supposedly cured my mom when she was ill.

If a tornado ever came to Hyde Park, I wondered if the Hood Witch would save the hood. My community was nothing like *The Wizard of Oz*, and neither was Hughley's replica of the country farm that the tornado ruined. I was surprised his tornado glass tank didn't break.

His best class demonstration was the time he used his weather machine to create lightning. It reminded me of what happened the first time I saw The Light. The way that the lightning from the machine illuminated a single space of darkness reminded me how electricity comes from out of thin air.

After showing us how lightning works, Hughley captured a volt of electricity inside a giant glass globe. Then he explained to us what happens when gases and electrodes mix together once they're placed inside a vacuum, which led to a lecture about how plasma balls worked.

He explained how plasma is a heated gas that contains equal amounts of energy called ions and electrons. While ions are atoms and molecules filled with positive electricity, electrons are small particles of matter occupied by negative light. A plasma ball is a clear glass vacuum crowded with noble gas and negative and positive electricity, while strands of plasma extend from a smaller glass orb inside the ball called an electrode to the glass whenever electricity is supplied, creating fascinating beams of colored light.

Hughley gave each member of the class an eight-inch plasma ball as a gift. Although they weren't as large as the one in class, they still were decent in size—as big and circular as a honeydew melon. I called it a "lightning ball." It sat on top of a triangular base and ran off solar energy. There wasn't a cord to plug it in.

I took the ball home and used it as a nightlight. I was glad it didn't float across my room or try to speak to me when I was asleep. It looked cool in the dark, and I couldn't stop staring at it. It gave off a beautiful assortment of waves and colors and paintings of light that made it seem as if it was a circular aquarium filled with energy instead of water, and eventually The Light got jealous. The night I brought it home, The Light appeared to hover next to the ball, sizing it up as if it was a living object that had control of its own appearance.

"Why did you bring it home? It's not that special," she said.

"I brought it home because my teacher gave it to me, and plus I like it. What does it matter to you?"

"It doesn't matter nothing to me at all," The Light said, sounding perturbed, before vanishing into thin air.

A week went by without me seeing The Light. I figured that it must've still been jealous of the ball I brought home. I thought I would never see The Light again, and Hughley's gift would take its place.

CHAPTER 18

# DEATH OF A LIGHTNING BALL

90

One morning, I woke up and noticed that the lightning ball no longer worked. I couldn't see any of the colorful light waves it once had, nor could I understand why it wouldn't power up if it ran from solar energy. I did everything to make it turn on: I shook it, yelled at it, repeatedly hit the power button, threw it on my bed, and spoke to it in a normal tone. I then figured that if it was sad, I could cheer it up. I talked to it using my boyhood charm. I cracked a few jokes, but it didn't laugh. So, I left the ball alone, hoping it might light up if it had a moment to itself, but that never happened. An entire week went by before I realized that the lightning ball was permanently dead.

I imagined the world where plasma balls come from. The one I had was a ruler of its own kind, and as soon as all the other lightning globes heard of its death they would announce "the king is dead," before shouting "long live the king!" A smaller glass ball would fill with plasma until it was big enough to take its place as an exalted monarch in The Land of Glowing Orbs, similar to a prince in *The Legend of Robinhood* story where King Richard the Lionheart passes away.

Unfortunately, since the globe wouldn't turn on, there was only one other thing left for me to do. I took the ball back to Mr. Hughley one morning before class and asked if he could give me a new one. He checked out the ball to figure out the problem, but he couldn't find any solutions. He told me there was nothing he could do—he had no more balls.

"I'm all out, Demetrius."

"Aw, man," I said. "I need another one. It helps me sleep better at night."

Hughley handed me back the ball. "Keep this as a souvenir. As soon as I get more, you'll be the first to have one. I promise."

"I guess," I said, shrugging my shoulders. I was heading toward my seat when the school bell rang. Kids began pouring into class. I took a seat and placed the plasma lamp on top of my desk.

Later, when it was time for recess, I took the ball with me when I went outside.

CHAPTER 19

# THAT STORY ABOUT THE GLOWING POTATO

Once upon a time in a land called Ireland, there was a man in Connaught named Baxter Madison Quinn. He was the son of a ginger-headed Irishman who taught him everything he knew about potato growing, and it paid off. Baxter inherited his father's hair color, and his gift for agriculture. The potatoes he grew were huge and robust. He became a successful sharecropper during the 1830s until the Great Famine in 1845, which was caused by late blight, a disease that destroys the leaves and edible roots of the potato plant.

Though there were hopes that a good crop would arrive, diseased potatoes from the previous harvest sprouted bad shoots. When harvest time came around the following season, the blight struck, spreading fifty miles per week across the countryside, destroying every potato in Ireland. Baxter's crops were ruined. Each potato he split open had soft, dark spots that covered its insides. His family had no choice but to eat soup at the soup kitchen. There, farmers exchanged stories about good times.

Baxter Madison Quinn was my Great-Great-Grandma Cindy's father. She was a nine-year-old by the time those ruined potato crops took Ireland into a famine. Cindy and her family came close to starving to death plenty of times; they were lucky to eat twice a week.

93

One night, Cindy was playing outside the barn when she saw a mysterious light. It was big and round like a crystal ball, and it popped out of nowhere, floating in the center of the dark barn, just like The Light I saw in my room. This glowing ball spoke like a young girl, just like mine. She asked Cindy if she wanted to play a game.

"Yes," Cindy said. She was too afraid to say no.

The Light asked her to close her eyes. Cindy complied.

"Hold out both of your hands," The Light said. "Now, place them together. Make sure they are in the best shape of a bowl you can make. And promise me. No peeking," The Light said.

"No peeking, I swear. Are you going to treat me with something to eat? A tad famished, I am. Would do anything for a piece of soda bread. Me stomach's been growling like a wicked beast with a stinging wound for almost the entire day. Do you know where I could get extra soup without being a burden?"

"I have something better than soup," The Light said.

"Let me have it, please!" Cindy kept her eyes closed like she promised. She was smiling from ear to ear.

"Now, open your eyes," The Light said.

Cindy opened her eyes and looked down at what she was now holding in her hand.

She held a glowing potato with an intensity that shone brighter than the orb. Her green eyes filled with amazement. She couldn't believe what she was seeing. "What is this?" she said.

"Isn't it obvious? It's a glowing potato," The Light said.

"I know, but what—"

"You're to do what I tell you," The Light replied.

"And what is that?" Cindy asked, caressing the rough, warm surface of the potato, staring at it while it glowed in her palm.

The Light then gave her instructions. The name of the game was "Hide the Potato." To play the game, you dug a hole in the ground and buried a rotten potato.

First, Cindy found a shovel in one corner of the barn and made her way out into the empty potato field. There, The Light told her to dig a hole deeper than the entire length of herself before throwing the glowing potato into the pit. She had to cover the hole with enough dirt to bury the spud.

As soon as she finished, the ground shook. Dead potato plants sank into the ground, one by one, until none were still around. A bright beam of light shone through each of the holes they left behind.

Cindy became afraid and ran into the farmhouse to tell her father what happened. She didn't care if she got in trouble for sneaking out. Her father threw on his clothes and they both returned to the field to an amazing  sight. Spuds were piled high as a mountain, right in the spot where Cindy planted the glowing potato.

The next morning, the Irish Famine was over. New crops of potatoes sprouted all over the country.

# CHAPTER 20

# DON'T CALL ME CHINESE

96

Bob's Market was a small, run-down corner store about a block from where I lived. It was the only place in the neighborhood that sold money orders. My mother sent me there every month when it was time to pay the rent.

The store owner was Mr. Bob, a bald, middle-aged Korean man who stood about average height. Mr. Bob had a round face that reminded me of a smiling moon man. He usually wore denim jeans and a t-shirt with an unbuttoned, short-sleeved flannel shirt. He was the coolest, gentlest guy in the neighborhood. Mr. Bob would sometimes give store credit to folks in the hood that needed food to get by. Other times, the hood would get to him, and it was funny to watch him get angry. He would always call the black kids "little hip-hops" and "little rappers." I guess it was better than calling us all little niggers.

"Come on, Mr. Bob! Can I get a money order, please? My momma needs it. She has to pay the rent," I pleaded, standing in front of the counter one day after school.

Mr. Bob stood behind the cash register smiling, until it became clear to him what I was asking. His face completely dropped. Now, he looked like a moon man that had the burden of delivering bad news.

"Sorry, little hip-hop, this not going to work this time. Food stamps are only for buying food! Nothing else!"

"Come on, Mr. Bob, please!" I begged. It was the first of the month, and we really needed the money. "Just do this for us one time, sir. You let us trade stamps for other things before."

"The answer is no. Get your little rapper ass out of my store!" he said, in a serious tone, pointing toward the door.

"I'm not a rapper. Why you call me that?"

"All of you people are rappers. If you listen to rappers, then you are a rapper, like Dr. Dre and Snoopy Doggy Dog," he said.

"His name is Snoop Doggy Dog."

"Okay, but I still can't trade money orders for food stamps. You must have cash. I'm sorry."

"How is my mother going to pay the rent?"

"Not my problem, kid."

Mr. Bob went to tend the cash register, ignoring me as I continued my plea.

"Come on, Mr. Bob. It'll be the last time you will ever have to do my mother a favor."

Natalie's thug brother, sixteen-year-old Herman, walked through the door as I was talking to Mr. Bob. Herman was tall and lanky, standing about six foot two, and was slender, with the same hair and dark caramel skin his sister had. I liked how he wore his hair faded with those big curls at the top. It made him look like that rapper, Special Ed, from the *I Got It Made* video. He was wearing a baggy hoodie and jeans. I was surprised to see him, afraid that he may be up to something. Supposedly, Herman had been robbing a lot of the stores in the area.

"What brings you in here, little man?" Herman said.

"Trying to get money orders for my mom," I said.

"So, he's not giving them to you?" Herman said, pointing over to Mr. Bob.

"He doesn't accept food stamps."

"Food stamps? For a money order? No, little homey, you need one of these if you want to get that act right." Herman lifted his hoodie to reveal a semi-automatic weapon.

I took a step back. I had never been that close to a gun.

"Don't move any further, little nigga," Herman said. Then he pulled out the gun and pointed it at Mr. Bob. "Give me all of your cash, Chinaman."

"Herman, no!" I said, taking a few steps away, ducking behind a rack of chips in a nearby aisle.

"I'm Korean, not Chinese!" Mr. Bob yelled, his hands in the air.

"I'm going to call your ass 'dead Korean asshole in a casket' if you keep talking, China. I'll show your ass what it means to be assaulted."

"The word is insulted. You should stay in school," Mr. Bob said.

"Assaulted. Insulted. Who gives a fuck? I'm tired of you chink motherfuckers coming to the hood and disrespecting the black man, like we're some type of joke. You always think we are trying to steal something out of your funky ass store," Herman yelled as he kept the gun pointed at Mr. Bob.

*Mr. Bob, please.* As I peeked above the shelf, I knew something bad was about to happen, but Mr. Bob just wouldn't stop adding his two cents.

"You are not a man. Robbing me is the same as stealing from my store. I never had a problem with you people," Mr. Bob said.

Herman put the gun closer to Bob's head, "Say something else, Buddha head."

"Allow the kid to leave. He doesn't need to see this." Mr. Bob looked over at me. "Do you still want those money orders?"

I nodded.

Herman gave me the okay to walk over. "Take what you need, little nigga, and get out of here," he ordered.

As Mr. Bob leaned over and handed me the money orders, he took my hand into both of his palms; his hands felt soft and smooth, and he had a blank look on his face. "Don't be a waste of life, like your silly friend. Take these money orders to your mom and let her know I said she can pay me back later."

"Okay," I said, dashing quickly out the door.

What I heard next was gunfire. Shots rang like the Fourth of July. I felt like I was Rambo, running skillfully out of a jungle war zone after a battle. When I got home, Momma was glad to get the money order and that I was okay. She had a hunch that something bad had happened, but I didn't tell her what went down.

The next day, I learned Mr. Bob survived. He had a gun holster concealed beneath his flannel shirt.

As for Herman, hopefully heaven had a ghetto filled with stores to rob.

# CHAPTER 21

# CALL THE PARAMEDICS

*Herman Peters*

was on my way to becoming the first black man he ever killed, and I hated myself for it. It wasn't my time to go. I swear to God on my momma that Korean nigga who shot me stood over me, checking me out and shit, all panicking and worrying if I would make it. The guy tried to do the right thing by taking a folded towel and pressing that shit against the shot wounds in my chest. "Why you have to be stupid?" he asked me.

I couldn't respond.

I felt tied up, trapped, and muzzled behind a locked door, watching the Korean store man talk to me and do all this shit to save me. Like I wanted to talk to him about the stuff I heard myself saying in my head. I could see him over me with tears in his eyes.

I felt his remorse. He told me he was "sorry" and not to fall asleep. He said I had to fight to stay alive.

I might have been young, and I may have stayed dumb, and I was an ignorant fool, but I'm smart enough to admit that my life wasn't worth my courage to survive. See, when your journey flashes before your eyes, it happens like a pre-recorded movie when someone fast-forwards on the VCR and the beginning,  middle, and end of what you are watching are all about you. The only other thing you want to do after that is push rewind; romanticizing sweet fantasies about the way you were born alive. If I had to keep it real, that's a very fucked up way to die.

A brother was conscious for like five minutes before everything went blank, and I heard my heart beating in my ears, throbbing slower with each pump of life striving through my veins. I wanted to tell him to "call the paramedics," but by the time he made the call, it was too late. Everything went black, and then I saw a bright light at the end of a narrow tunnel. Something then told me to keep walking toward it until I crossed over to the other side. I hoped somebody from my family was there to meet a nigga.

I had a lifetime to worry about my little sister.

*Natalie, I love you.*

# CHAPTER 22

# GONE BUT NOT FORGOTTEN

103

Three weeks passed before I saw Natalie again. She took Herman's death hard. I was surprised when I saw her show up at school. She commemorated his passing by wearing a picture of his smiling face on the front of her t-shirt. Below Herman's photo were words printed in white that read, "Never Forgotten." Underneath that were the years of Herman's birth and death, which memorialized his life span: "1976—1992."

Natalie's eyes were red from crying so much. Her hair hung free to the middle of her back. It was the first I ever saw her with her hair not worn in a bun or beneath a cap. Usually, she waited for me after school, but I saw her walking off by herself. It wasn't hard to understand why she didn't want to be bothered, but everyone could use a little cheering up, I figured. I had to run to catch up.

"Hey, Pretty Hair. You too good to wait up?" I said playfully.

"Sorry Dee, you know? Things been tough," she said.

"I understand." I walked along beside her, thinking there might be repercussions due to the information I was withholding. See, a part of me was feeling bad for being in the store with Herman moments before he got killed. Perhaps I could have talked him out of robbing the store. I never told Natalie I knew what happened; the only other person who knew I was there was Mr. Bob.

I had something that could have gotten Natalie's mind off things for a bit. During my art period, I made her a collage of Michael Jordan, her favorite basketball player. On one picture of MJ dunking, I had a picture of Herman's face pasted on the photo as Jordan's head. I took it out of my bag and gave it to Natalie.

She loved it. She stared at the picture, smiling ear to ear.

# CHAPTER 23

# THOU SHALL NOT KILL ME

105

Momma always told me to thank Geppetto for being born; I never did. I wanted him to die. With him out of the way, I knew I would spend fun times with my mom. She allowed me to watch some of her favorite horror films, like *Friday the 13th* and *Nightmare on Elm Street*.

My mother liked scary movies because she enjoyed seeing people's reactions to fear. She liked seeing what people did whenever danger was around. Her favorite villain was Freddy Kruger. She liked his stylish hat and his brown, bladed gloves. I was a fan of Jason and *Friday the 13th*. I liked his hockey mask and the relationship he had with his mom. They seemed close, as if they were the type to look out for one another. It kind of reminded me of Norman Bates and his mother in *Psycho*, and their creepy bond. Unconditional love, albeit in an evil way.

My favorite scene in *Friday the 13th* was when Jason's mother attempted to kill Alice, the camp counselor, after telling her she blamed her son's death on camp counselors who weren't watching him when he drowned. It was something I'd like to think my mom would do if that had happened to me. Unfortunately, Alice used a machete to decapitate Jason's mom. I didn't want anything like that happening to my mother, even though some nights she tried to kill me.

You see, every month, during her menstrual cycle, Geppetto would tell her to kill me since she was bleeding and couldn't make love with any of her sugar daddies. He told her that my dying would make the bleeding go away. One night, Momma tried to stab me when I was asleep. I had woken up from a bad dream as Godzilla and an army of tyrannosauruses were trying to eat me, and a talking dinosaur told me to wake up. There she was, hovering over my bed with a knife. She had an evil glare in her eye.

"Hello, son. I have a song about killing you. Like to hear it? Here it goes!" she said with the knife still held above me. She started singing as if she were a child reciting a nursery rhyme, "If you die, the birds will fly. That's why you have to go." And then she came down with the knife, only missing me by a second as I rolled away, hopped out of bed, and locked myself in the closet.

106

Another time, she threw a radio in the tub while I was taking a bath. I jumped out of the water, just fast enough. Then there were the times when Momma tried to poison me. Luckily, I knew the difference between the scents of Kool-Aid and radiator fluid. Sometimes, she would lie and say she poisoned my food just to scare me. Then she would laugh about it when she told me the truth. Luckily, she didn't always want me dead. Instead of killing me, she would take dope to ease the blue moods Geppetto would put her in.

"I get high every day, baby, because I love you. I don't want him to force me to do anything stupid. Only way I could get rid of him, baby, is to kill him. Momma don't want you to grow up and become a man alone," was what my mother always said.

"Thou shall not kill," was the only way I knew how to reply.

Whenever her illness was in check, we called her Good Geppetto, since her behavior wasn't so bad. She wouldn't try to kill me or even beat me up; instead, she would act like a partially normal, wiry drug addict with a sharp tongue.

I always tried to make sure she was on top of her medicine.

"Momma, did you take your medication?"

She would sigh, and tell me, "Did Jesus Christ paint the Mona Lisa?"

"No," I replied, handing her a glass of water and a couple of pills that were supposed to keep her calm from her medicine bottle. "Leonardo da Vinci painted the Mona Lisa, Momma. Well, at least that's what my art teacher told me. Do you know who helped Jesus carry the cross?"

"Oh, so you don't think I read the Bible, huh? Simon of Cyrene's the one who helped Jesus," Momma said as she finally took the pills.

# CHAPTER 24

# KICKBALL

At my school, the primary sport played during recess was kickball. Kickball was like baseball, but instead of using a bat, you used your feet to kick a rubber ball as far out into the field as you could. The standard balls were large as soccer balls, and those are the ones we preferred the most. Though some children like Ray-Ray from special needs class had a thing for oversized balls. He loved the sound they made when they smacked against the pavement and got on everybody's nerves. No one ever wanted to play with Ray-Ray. He always peed and boo-booed himself and would still wear white pants, but that is beside the point.

The rules of kickball were the same as baseball, except a player could also throw the ball at someone as a way of giving them an "out" when they were not touching a base. There were no strikes and no errors, and the teachers were the umpires. We had an infield and an outfield, and up to eleven people were allowed to play on each team. Every crew had to have at least four girls on their squad. The worst players got picked last, and I was continuously one of the kids that got chosen first.

Our kickball field wasn't a traditional turf with green grass. It was a full concrete basketball court that was converted into a yellow, chalk-drawn, diamond-shaped playing ground with four bases and a home plate, which looked more like a diagram a builder would have had sketched before building the actual field. The stretch of the "field" went from east to west between two traditional basketball hoops. We had an outfield and infield. Center court was the pitcher's mound. I loved kickball and usually played at recess, but on the day I had the plasma globe, I took it out with me and sat on a bench near the field while all the other kids played. I stared at the lightning ball, wondering why it wasn't working any longer.

The best player out of all the kids in the fourth grade was Jamari. Everybody gave Jamari the nickname Shaka, since the South African biopic *Shaka Zulu* was his favorite TV mini-series, and like the character from the motion picture, Jamari didn't like wearing shoes, no matter the occasion. Shaka was excellent at playing kickball barefoot.

One time, he kicked the ball so hard it went over the playground's tall metal gate and rolled down Hyde

Park Boulevard until it got to Crenshaw. I didn't believe it, even if that was the cackle everybody was spreading. Shaka loved confirming the rumor. On this day, I heard him bragging to a group of kids about making the kickball go over the gate. I said what I thought out loud, not caring if he heard me—he had got my attention, and I no longer paid attention to the lightning ball.

"Shaka, you lie too much. Who could kick a ball that hard?"

"I could kick a ball that hard. My daddy was in the Marines, and he knows karate. All his kicking power was passed down to me."

"Fool, please, you don't even take karate lessons."

"I don't need lessons. I was born a black belt. If you was man enough, I could teach you something."

"You ain't no man."

"I'm more man than you," Shaka replied. "I got hair coming in up under my arms and on my thing-thing."

All the boys standing nearby laughed. The girls were grossed out, especially Natalie. She rolled her eyes and chimed in, "Ew, you said hair was coming in on your thing-thing. Boy, bye! That sounds like a personal problem. Ain't nobody want to hear all that."

"Ain't nobody asked you about what you want to hear," Shaka said. "You can just shut up."

"Shut don't go up, punk," Natalie exclaimed, sounding and looking annoyed.

"Well, shut it down, then. Stay in a girl's place."

"Oh, heck no!" Natalie was revved up. She started heading over toward Jamari to get in his face and talk more smack, but I stopped her.

"He's not worth it," I said.

"Uh, yeah he is!" Natalie said.

I looked her in the eye and told her, "It'll be okay. I got this."

Shaka teased the both of us. "Look at Demetrius, trying to protect his girlfriend. Funny thing, I can't tell which one is the girl and which one's the boy."

That really got me agitated. "Shaka, I am not the boy." I got in his face. "I'm the man. I'll tear your behind up in a kickball game, too."

"You don't want none of this."

"I want it all."

Shaka smiled as if he already knew he won. "Let's make a bet. If I lose, I'll come to school dressed like M.C. Hammer. I'll even dance like him, too."

"And?"

"And … if I win, you got to let me have that little dumb lightning ball you keep carrying around."

"My lightning ball?"

"Yeah, stupid. Your lightning ball."

I looked at the ball and thought about whether I should or shouldn't. I ended up figuring I should. The ball wasn't even working anymore, so what was the point of trying to keep it?

The next morning during recess, we played that game, and oh boy was it a game.

# CHAPTER 25

# THE MAGICAL OTHERSIDE

113

The teams for kickball were six on six, and Shaka and I were captains of each squad. I choose Nats, a couple of boys, and then another girl. Although Nats was good at kicking, she was terrible at allowing her foot to connect with the ball or let her feet hit the pavement quickly enough to run fast with nobody chasing behind her. Her speed came with a circumstance. The other kids I chose were Ray-Ray and Marcus, and that day, Ray-Ray was a little more Ray-Ray than usual in those infamous white pants because not only did he use the bathroom on himself that morning, he refused to go to the nurse's office and change. That brown streak on the back of his pants was disgusting. I still gag thinking about it.

Marcus was a regular kid like me, except he probably had a normal mom and no issues of having a dad who provided a stable home. Although, that is beside the point. I never was jealous. The other player was a girl named Hermina, who stuttered a lot. The older kids called her Hermina Munster because she was tall for a fourth grader and had big feet. Her mother always bought her shoes that looked like the shiny boots Herman Munster wore on the TV show *The Munsters*. Hermina always wore slicked bangs over a greasy, funny-shaped forehead that resembled a permanent flat top that seemed to be more skeletal than just a simple hairstyle meant for a boy.

Nats, Hermina, and I were the outsiders of the fourth grade; I would consider Ray-Ray an outsider, but he was also an outsider to our group. The school staff always made us play with him. I didn't want to pick Ray-Ray because if he weren't the first to kick, he'd throw a tantrum. So Ray-Ray kicked first, and his anticipation danced with excitement.

"Slowball, I want a slowball."

I told him, "It's the slowest it can go, Ray-Ray."

"No, it's not," he said. "If they can't play right, I'm telling that they're cheatin'."

To Ray-Ray, cheating would be rolling the ball so fast he couldn't kick it. The pitcher on Shaka's team complied and gave Ray-Ray a slowball.

For some reason, Ray-Ray must've thought he was the main star in a soccer game and up to kick against the goalie or something. Who knows? But all I knew is that he started dancing around the kicker's mound like he was the star athlete in a major ball game, pointing out into the centerfield and looking at the pitcher, Shaka, dead in the eye, saying, "This ball's gonna fly over your head, so watch out, stupid."

When the ball came rolling, Ray kicked it as hard as he could. The ball went out far enough into middle field for Ray to make it to first base. "Told you. Ball went over your head!" Ray-Ray said to Shaka.

"You did good, Ray-Ray," I said.

Shaka smirked. "Both of y'all be quiet. That ball  didn't go nowhere. Ray-Ray got lucky."

"No, I didn't," he argued.

The bases were loaded by the time it was my turn to kick. Shaka teased me, saying my kick wouldn't be good. I kicked the ball hard with every bit of my might and it soared straight up into sky like a spaceship going into orbit, twirling and expanding from the size of a kickball to a giant beach ball as it changed colors and glowed. It stayed in the sky, hovering as if it had control of itself and didn't want to come down. I glanced over at the bench and didn't see my plasma lamp sitting on its triangular base. It became obvious the lamp got kicked into the sky.

Everyone's mouth grew more agape as the ball twirled faster and changed colors and then textures. It was now changing from a rubber ball into a translucent orb with electricity inside it. It pulsated energy waves from its nucleus, which stuck and randomly pulled away from the clear glass-like inner surface. The sky turned black, then thunder came rumbling before it preluded a flash of brightness and lightning struck the ball, hitting it the same way the volts of electricity had done in Mr. Hughley's demonstration during science period, except this lightning seemed to be energizing the sphere, sucking away power left in the sky. Several pigeons fell to the ground lifeless before the orb exploded. The other birds flew away. The sky went back to normal and pieces of hard Jolly Rancher's candy fell onto the kickball field. I thought I was daydreaming until I heard one kid say, "Wow, what was that?"

I picked up one of the Jolly Rancher's and ate it. I immediately fell to the ground. Then everything went black. I stood over my body, watching myself as I laid on the ground without breathing.

Natalie screamed, "Dee!"

I came over and stood next to her, trying to get her attention. I wanted to respond but couldn't.

"He needs help." Natalie motioned for one of the campus aides to come over. "I don't know what happened. He just fell," Natalie said.

The campus aide confirmed I wasn't breathing. She tried to resuscitate me until the paramedics came. She even tried CPR, which I thought was gross. Her mouth over mine? *Yuck!*

Natalie stood next to where I was lying. "Get up, Dee. Come on, man."

The aide overheard her. "He isn't going to get up," she said. "Kids, I need everyone to step back. Allow the paramedics to do their job."

The children backed away, all watching what was happening to me. "I can't find a pulse," said one paramedic as they spoke amongst themselves. They quickly rushed and opened my shirt and placed defibrillator pads on my chest. "Ready? Clear!" *VOMP!* "Nothing ..." The paramedics couldn't get a pulse. "Let's try again."

Natalie looked worried.

I stood next to her watching everything that was happening, "What do you think is wrong with me?" I asked.

Natalie didn't respond. She stood there in shock. She had tears in her eyes. The campus aide came over and consoled her. "It will be alright, precious. I know he's your friend." The other kids like Shaka, Marcus, Hermina, and even Ray-Ray came over and tried to make Nats feel better. They walked past me like I wasn't even there. I tried to get their attention.

"Dang, guys, it's not that bad. I'm standing right here, look." I waved my arms, thinking that would get their attention, but it didn't. "Hey, I am right here for crying out loud."

Still no response.

"Is this supposed to be funny?" I said. I walked over to where the paramedics had me, still trying to find a pulse. My face looked pale and I could tell I wasn't breathing but knew that whatever had happened to me couldn't have been that bad because I was standing over myself watching the paramedics trying to bring me back to consciousness. I even had a few ideas to try to help. I tried to get the attention of a paramedic. "Sir, excuse me, sir, if you put some water on my face, maybe I'll get up. I've seen on a couple of TV shows where they gave guys smelling salts to wake them up. You probably could try that." I tapped the paramedic on the shoulder. "Hello, mister, can you hear me?"

The paramedic ignored me.

I ended up getting closer to where my body was, tapping myself on the shoulder, trying to awake myself. "Hey, get up. Come on, Dee!" Then that's when I saw the paramedic look up from his nearby defibrillator monitor and tell his partner, "We have a pulse."

*FLASH!*

\* \* \*

"Hello!"

All I heard back was an echo. I felt stranded in the dark tunnel I was now standing in. An opening at the end of the passageway appeared, blaring a bright light. Something inside me told me to walk through the warm brightness of the portal, and I was glad I did. On the other side, I met ancestors from my mother's side of the family, and I didn't want to come back, as it felt good to have a love that was normal. However, they told me I had to go back to what they called the "natural world," as it wasn't my time to cross to the Other Side and I was only there in the afterlife to say hello to family members I had never met, and, my mother needed me.

I was told to "wake up."

I heard my heartbeat pounding in my ears. I felt my body being yanked back into the playground and thrown onto a stretcher while cold plastic blew cool air into my covered nose and face. My skin crawled at the slam of a metal door before I passed out and ambulance sirens rushed me to the hospital.

Hovering above my bed were concerned faces that belonged to my mother and Aunt Charlene. A wet kiss from my mom pressed against my cheek. Charlene was delicate as her smile when she saw I was awake. She squeezed my shoulder and told me, "Glad to have you back, Honey Bear."

Momma was the opposite with an ugly crying face and tears in her eyes; she reached across the bed and hugged me. "Thank you, Jesus, for bringing back my baby. My sweet light of the universe." My mother looked me in the eye. "Don't ever scare me like this again. Okay?"

I brushed a tear away from her cheek and told her, "I love you too, Momma."

When the doctor walked in, he told Momma and Auntie that I may have passed out because of dehydration, and it was important to make sure I was drinking enough water, and that I was free to go home.

# CHAPTER 26

# SHAPESHIFTERS

A t night, when the lights were out, our hallway became a corridor filled with candlelit darkness. Momma believed the lit candles protected her from the shadows on the walls that were there to kill her. She called the shadows "shapeshifters." Geppetto created them. He used them as his minions, the same way Lucifer used demons. The only difference was that he believed in walking the line between good and evil. Geppetto thought corruption was a ruler of goodness, and darkness was the shadow of light.

Shapeshifters were reflections of the human soul. They could transform into the silhouette of any object or living thing. Then, from a profile, they could become actual people. Momma always advised me to be careful anytime I dealt with a shapeshifter. One shapeshifter she despised was Adella James, a child service worker that came to our house after someone in our building complained about Momma being an unfit mother.

One morning, Ms. Adella knocked on the door and strode into our apartment, sitting on the couch directly across from my mother. Momma was dressed in a red low-cut blouse and light blue jean shorts, her dreads tied back in a ponytail. I watched them through the crack of my bedroom door. Ms. Adella wore a tight-fitted, dark blue pants suit. Her demeanor was stern and abrasive, probably ex-military. You could tell she was the type of person who had to be in charge, regardless of the circumstance. Momma hated the "take charge" types. They reminded her of Geppetto.

"So … Olivia," Adella said, taking out her pen and clipboard to jot stuff down.

Momma keyed in. "Is this an interview? Why are you here? And you can call me Ms. Jordan."

"We'll get to that in a second, but first things first. There's some information I need from you."

"What information?" Momma's voice swelled.

Anytime she was infuriated, Momma would clap her hands as a representation for every word she said.

Are you a miss or missus?" Adella asked.

My mother was boiling. Her hands got to clapping. They slapped together ten times for a total of ten words. "Bitch! How many s's have you heard roll off my tongue?"

"About as many s's as there are in the word stereotype. So, I guess one."

"Take it and stick it where the sun won't shine and the flowers don't grow. Bougie ho!" Momma glared at the worker with a hard, repulsed look on her face. It would have been impossible for Adella not to catch the vibe.

"Ms. Jordan, I'm here because I received several complaints that you might be abusing your child. Is that true?"

Hearing the word "abusing" caused me to quiver.

"That's a bald-faced lie. How could I be abusing my only son?"

"You tell me. How could you be abusing your child, Ms. Jordan? I have complaints saying that there has been a lot of screaming and fighting come from this apartment."

"Geppetto said it's a part of the boy's growing up," she blurted out.

My mother got nervous when she lied. It was something she wasn't good at. She always stuck to the truth, which did her no right.

"Who is Geppetto?" Adella replied.

"Who is Geppetto?" Momma said, stunned, as if she was surprised Adella didn't know the answer.

I knew I had to save her. It was like watching someone drown, and you want to prevent them from going under the water a second time. I darted out into the living room as if I was a lawyer filing a motion in court.

"Geppetto is just a family friend!" I said, hoping my response would work.

The look on Ms. Adella's face showed the sheer example of discernment. Doubt would be a better word. "A family friend, huh?" she said, watching me sit on the couch next to my mother.

"You heard the boy, a family friend," my mother said, beaming and putting her arm around me.

Adella jotted more things down on her clipboard. It was like she was stalling until she found the perfect time to push the right button. I sat on the couch, watching.

Adella went in for the kill. "Where's the boy's father?" She spoke as if she knew my mother didn't know the answer.

*Yeah, where was my father?*

My mother looked at me while collecting her thoughts. It was like she knew she had to be careful what she said next, or perhaps it was just her merely not letting me in on the big secret.

"His father is somewhere that stinks."

"And where is that exactly?" Ms. Adella was stunned.

Momma gets up, stomping her feet, clapping out the words, "Up your ass, bitch! Get out of my house. Dyke ho. I see you looking at my titties."

"Girl, don't flatter yourself. You are not my type. And it's obvious you conceived out of wedlock."

"Get out of my house with your stupid ass!" My mother pointed at the door.

I got up off the couch and did the same exact thing, copying my momma. "Yeah! Get out of our house, stupid ole lady with your dumb self!"

Adella paused, taking a moment, stunned at what she was seeing. "Splendid little boy, isn't he?" She got up from the couch and headed toward the door.

Momma followed, and I was there nearby in tow. "Touché, heifer," she said. "You're talking above our heads. I give it to you." Momma stood there with her hand on her hip, prepared to take the fire of anything the social worker had to say next.

"Give me what, exactly? It's sisters like you that  give us a bad name," Adella said, turning around after reaching the other side of the doorway with her back toward the hall. Then she gave Momma a stern look. "If I hear any more complaints about you abusing or not properly taking care of your son, I'll make sure he's removed from your custody, indefinitely. You know what indefinitely means, don't you?"

"Bitch, I've already told you. You're talking above my head! I'm down here!" she gestured. "Your mouth is up there!" she said, using her hands to mark off a point where all her smart-mouthed talking was going. "All that yapping you're doing ain't nothing but water. I'm drowning, bitch. See, what you need is to make like a boat and float your weird polyester man pantsuit wearing ass up out of here, ole miserable heifer. Float out, bitch!" Momma slammed the door.

I gave her a nudge. "That point goes to Momma!"

"No, baby," she said as she shook her head.

My mother brushed the left side of my face with the back of her right hand. She used the same hand to grab my chin and lift my face. Then she put it a little toward the right, finding the perfect spot for a kiss on the cheek. She looked me straight in the eye. "That point goes for us. I'll never allow anyone to break up our home. Not her, not Geppetto, or anyone else. I would rather be dead. You understand?"

I nodded my head. I knew what she meant, but hearing Adella say my mother abused me was something different. I thought all kids my age got punished by their parents. I thought everyone's momma starved, punched, and tried to kill them.

That was a thing I had yet to understand.

CHAPTER 27

# PUPPET MASTER

S
ome nights, when she played music loud, it sounded like a party happening in Momma's room, like a hired DJ spinning her nonsense on turntables that would never scratch or skip a beat. There was a poetry to her rhetoric, a melody to her mayhem; her cusswords were fight music.

"Shit. Damn. Motherfucker. Sit down before I kick your ass," is what she screamed in her sleeping chambers.

Her words banged through the walls as if they were a sequence of punches being thrown to her soul. As I listened from my bedroom, unseen body blows and uppercuts left a soreness in my memory. My thoughts were contusions.

She no longer wanted to be his puppet. "Stop trying to control me, like some damn wooden boy. I am not your wooden girl!" she said, screaming at the top of her lungs. "Leave me alone!" she said. "I will not allow them to kill me. Keep them the fuck away, Puppet Master!"

This was something he hated being called. It reminded him of the time he worked with an Italian circus as a puppeteer. There, he slaved for food and shelter, using his only son as a wooden puppet. Pinocchio was his name.

"Guess you know what it feels like to walk in a black man's shoes," she'd scream. "Your son is dead. He was made of wood. My boy is made of flesh. I have a son to raise. Black boys without fathers come a dime a dozen."

Anytime she fought with Geppetto, it was hard to tell who was wrong. I never saw it as a problem; I just thought that was how violence and chaos got along. Stillness was the escape I found inside myself. I'd close my eyes and take a deep breath, blocking out the noise around me. I'd fall asleep under the covers, comfortable, like a frog in a well.

# CHAPTER 28

# A HOUSE OF GAS

**W**henever Mom argued with Geppetto, the wall on the side of her bedroom would shake, causing all the candles outside her room to rock back and forth as if they were going to fall onto the carpet and burn. She often had a vision that she would die, burned alive by flames. A voice in her thoughts visualized our apartment combusting. The storyteller that spoke inside her told her everyone in the building would die from smoke inhalation.

One time, when cooking eggs for breakfast, she thought the blaze underneath the pan was trying to attack her. She used orange juice to put out the burners on top of the stove. It seemed she knew there was a bomb that was about to explode.

The inferno on the stove reminded her of her vision. The red and orange of the fire was the reason her head spun. Smoke was the breath of Lucifer. The Devil's air was poison and filled with toxins made by Geppetto himself. That was the way fire killed you.

"God made fire so no man would touch it," my momma said, letting me know that was the reason why she lit the last candle on the dresser in the hall outside of her room very carefully. "This is dangerous," she said.

"If it's dangerous, why you do it?" I said.

"To remind myself I don't have to worry about the future," she said. "You understand?"

"No," I said, honestly. Living with my mother was like raising a child of my own. You had to always be there to protect her from danger. She was like one of those kids who had to have their hands slapped away from a hot stove. She almost burned me with that iron, yet there had been times where she kept me safe from being burned by the oven. We were like two kids with a box of matches, trapped inside a house filled with gas.

After that, my mother never cooked me a meal that required fire. Applejacks and sandwiches were all she made.

CHAPTER 29

# WAS 1 AFRAID?

One night, when The Light appeared, floating over my bed as usual, it asked me if I was afraid of death. I told The Light I didn't know. Even though Momma tried to kill me, and Mr. Bob killed Herman when he attempted to rob the store, and there were those dead dogs in the alley, the only thing I knew about life was living. I learned about death through movies and comic books, like when Doomsday killed Superman by beating him to death, and how often Batman and Spider-Man came close to dying. However, none of these were examples of how something naturally dies.

The Light lowered closer to me and told me it had bad news.

"Someone very close to you will pass away," The Light said.

"Who is that?"

"Who do you think?"

"Natalie?"

"Think again," The Light said.

"My mother?"

"Yeah, your mother will die, Demetrius."

I didn't know how to respond. It felt like my heart was another person beating the walls inside me while being trapped and yelling fire, and someone had to plunge their fist right through me to rip the life from my extinguished existence. If my soul had a shadow, it  would have lain dead and still, like the darkness that filled the room; blackness surrounded the ball of light that had now lowered itself closer to me.

The girl's face appeared for the second time. Her facial features were on the surface of the floating orb of light. She looked sad, like she really felt bad telling me about my mother's death. "I need you to be strong when it happens," The Light said.

"But ..." I couldn't finish my sentence.

"I'm so sorry, Demetrius," she said as I woke up in a cold sweat.

The next moment there was a blink of light.

*FLASH!*

# CHAPTER 30

# WILLIE EARL

After hearing noises coming from the hall, I went into my mother's room, and there he was, nude and lying next to her—not Geppetto himself, but our apartment manager, Willie Earl. He was the sugar daddy I hated the most. I didn't like the way he spoke to me, gritting his false teeth. I also hated the way he left his teeth in a glass on the nightstand closest to his side of the bed. One time, when the dentures were removed from the glass, I mistook it for a glass of fresh water and drank it to quench my thirst. When I found out it was his glass for the false teeth, I came close to throwing up.

I shook the mattress on my mother's side of the bed. She woke up, then covered herself with a blanket and moved to the edge of the bed, leaving Willie snoring and exposed beside her.

"What's wrong, baby?" my mother said.

133

"I saw The Light. It was trying to show me something," I said.

"Poor baby. Come here." My mother leaned over; I could tell by the look on her face that she saw fear in my eyes. "What did it show you?"

"It showed me you were going to die."

"Die? Die, like how?

I shrugged. "I don't know. It was a bad dream. I woke up and ran out the room."

My mother grabbed me and held me tight in her naked bosom. It was very awkward, but it was her way of showing me she was there to protect me. She kissed me on the forehead, and I started to feel better. "It'll be okay, doo-doo bear."

"Will it?" I said.

"Remember, I told you the universe will always be there to look after you, whenever I am not around … hmm? You are my child. God knows that."

"The Light would never come in here. Can I sleep with you?"

Still lying naked in bed without a blanket to cover the ashiest parts of his body, ole Willie Earl rolled over and chimed in, wrinkled balls and all. Willie was one of those ex-veterans who lost half of their mind in Vietnam and another half of themselves somewhere on a disco floor in the early seventies after snorting too many lines of cocaine and having too many bottles of Sparkling Cold Duck.

134

"Hell no. You little jive turkey-ass nigga. It's only going to be one dick in this bed tonight!"

"And it will not be yours!" my momma said, glaring at Willie Earl. "Ole ashy, hairy-ass-cheeks-having-ass motherfucker. Don't you ever talk to my son that way. I'll cut your dick off!"

"Hey ... hey goddamn it. Don't be playing with my dick."

"Don't be cussing at my son. Matter of fact, get your ass out of my bed!"

"But, Olivia?" Willie said, propping himself up. "You're going to make me leave? It's one o'clock in the morning. Don't kick me out, darling. Where I'm going to go, baby?"

"Back home ... across the hall to your ole bull-daggering wife. I see the way she be looking at me. I might let her sniff it if she knows how to treat a lady better than you. Bye, bye, Willie Earl," Momma said, getting out of bed and throwing on a robe. "Don't let the doorknob hit you."

"Can I see you tomorrow?"

"Bye, Willie."

And for some reason, I thought it was cool to chime in. "Bye, Willie."

Willie glared at me, gritting his false, overly white, mashed potato-looking-ass teeth, looking as drunk as Al Green trying to catch a beat, mouthing the words, "Fuck you, you little jive nigga," when my mother wasn't looking. As Willie bent over to pick up his clothes, he gyrated his hips in a thrusting back-and-forth disco motion, as if he was the shit-faced ghetto version of John Travolta in *Saturday Night Fever* shaking his ashy dick at me.

Willie headed to the bathroom. I watched him as he walked away, bony backside and all. I swear if I had a dollar for every time I saw Willie in my house naked, me and my mother would have enough money to buy a house in Windsor Hills.

After Willie left the room, my mother grabbed my chin, turning my face toward her. She looked at me like she was searching for an answer that was hiding in my eyes. "Don't you ever let me catch you treating a woman the way he treats me," she said. "I never had a husband, but sure damn well know that a real man never cheats on his wife. That's some shit little boys do. Do you understand your momma?"

"I guess."

"Let's go sleep in your room. Willie's nasty ass been laying in these sheets."

"Icky!" I said.

"Yeah, icky!"

We both laughed as we headed past the candles and shadows in the hall.

136

CHAPTER 31

# THE BITCH INSIDE THE MIRROR

*Olivia Jordan*

"Olivia! There is a naked little African American monster bitch inside of my mirror with a hairy pussy and small titties, and I think this weird, ditsy, itsy bitsy spider, Melba Moore-looking-ass bitch knows magic or something because this evil bitch always does something to make herself look like me, but the only difference between me and this raggedly-tail-ass heifer is that I don't need to shave my hairy-ass pussy. You need to put some hair relaxer on your vagina, bitch. Seriously, your pussy hairs are long and nappy, just like an afro. Stop staring at me, bitch. What are you looking at? Huh? Say something! Nasty bitch. If you don't like me, that's quite fine by me, ho. I don't like you. You fucking hussy," is what I told that smoked-out, crack rock, J.J. Fad, Vanity Six looking-ass bitch. Ole drippy, Jheri-curl-wearing, Eazy-E, face-having-ass, ho. I wasn't fucking around—that bitch needed to keep her freaky ass the fuck out of my freaking mirror. Looking at my pussy and shit.

I took the bucket of black paint I had and smeared it all over her stupid ass until I couldn't see her standing in the mirror anymore. I black plagued her stupid ass. Dumb bitch copying my moves and shit. She could have at least put on some damn drawers and rubbed some lotion on those crusty-ass, raisin nipple titties.

"Skinny, evil bitch! Fuck you!"

"Fuck you, too!" said the bitch inside the mirror.

I heard a young bitch's voice from across the room. It could've been a ghost, or my imagination. Maybe it was one of God's fuck angels that came down from heaven to fuck with me, but whatever or whoever the fuck it was, it sounded like a little girl.

"Stop with all that cussing, Lydia."

"Who in the fuck said that? Stop cussing? Bitch, who in the fuck is you to crawl up the cat's pussy and strike a match? Shit, I must be higher than a motherfucker, tripping off some shit. What's that noise? Is anybody there? Huh? Demetrius, is that you? Take your little nosy, stumpy ass back to bed, boy. Don't need nobody else fucking with me when I am asshole naked and high. Too bad I can't say the same for the ugly-ass bitch that keeps fucking with me in the mirror. I'm going to smear this black paint all over that stupid bitch, so she can't see none of this fine ass. Ole dyke-ass hoe."

"Stop with all that cussing, Lydia. Mother didn't raise us to have such a foul mouth."

"My name is Olivia! Who in the fuck are you to call me out of my name, bitch?"

"It's me, Lydia."

"Don't call me Lydia. No one knows me by that name. How do you know me?"

"What do you mean, how do I know you? I know you very, very well, Lydia. It's me," she said, calmly.

"Who in the fuck are you? I must be higher than a giraffe's eyebrows. I don't even know who in the fuck 'you' are. Why you fucking with me?"

"Lydia ..."

"Shit ..." I recognized the voice. *God, please don't let it be her!* I prayed to keep the past behind me. *I don't need her in my life.*

"Please, don't say that, Lydia." Her voice thundered in a low rumble.

"Oh, no! It's her, I know it is. And that bitch from the mirror is here to kill me. Is anyone her to protect me? Momma! Jesus! Somebody!" I yelled.

"No one will kill you, Lydia. The only bitch in the mirror is you. I'm just here to say hello. There is no need to bring Momma into it, and I'm pretty sure God doesn't like ugly, especially when it's naked."

My body trembled. I was so scared I peed on that ole janky-ass floor of mine.

"You don't remember your twin sister, Lydia? You don't remember the games we used to play when we were little? Lydia—"

"Don't call me that!" I said. "I'm not here, that's not my name no more. We traded, and you promised. Why you've got to be such a selfish little bitch? You fucking whore!" I shouted as I took a few steps back from where  the voice of this little demon bitch was coming from.

"Aw, Lydia. You are still such a potty mouth. I love you too much to hate you."

## CHAPTER 32

# THE GIRL FROM THE LIGHT

"Hello. Do you want to play a game?"

One night, when I woke up to go to the bathroom, I saw a crack of light spilling into my room from beneath my door, and as usual, my room was dark. I heard Momma in the living room yelling and cussing. I assumed she was either fussing at Geppetto or one of her sugar daddies. It had been a while since she saw Willie Earl. I couldn't shake that image of him standing stark naked in front of me from out of my head. So, if my mother were in the next room yelling at him, I wouldn't have been surprised.

"Get the fuck out of my house, Olivia! Why are you here?" she said. "What do you want from me? Why can't you just leave me alone?"

After hearing that, I knew it was going to be one of those nights where I had to hold my pee, and I really had to go. I mean really, really go. I had to rock back and forth, bouncing in place, while using my free hand to cover that small area of my bladder. I was about to spray fluid like a fire hose. I did the "pee-pee dance" to fight the urge. Momma's yelling got louder.

I opened the door quietly to see what was happening out in the living room. Momma was standing in the middle of the floor, stark naked, near a sizeable makeshift mirror she kept in the hallway. Directly in front of her was the girl that lived inside The Light. It was the first time I saw her out of her silhouette and outside the orb. The Light girl had taken on the form of my mother's childhood twin sister and wore a taffeta dress from all the family photos. I had recognized her voice and remained frozen. The only thing I could do is watch what happened next. I had wondered how Momma was going to react towards the girl from The Light.

"Remember the game we used to play?" the girl said, staring at Momma without breaking eye contact.

I was surprised Momma didn't respond right away. She just stood there, nervous, trembling. It was the first time I saw her afraid.

# CHAPTER 33

# YOUR SISTER'S KEEPER

*Olivia Jordan*

"Leave me alone, Olivia!" I yelled, stumbling across the room, trying my fucking best to get away from that little blasted bitch after I saw her hiding inside that bright light she always hid in when she came around to fuck with me. Twisted little tramp couldn't have given a freaking shit if I had any piece of sanity left after going through what I went through. She wanted me to suffer because I was alive. She wanted me to suffer because she was jealous. I could eat, shit, change my period pads, fuck, and smell the rotten odor of life's death lingering like poisoned air. My once sweet sister Olivia knew I should have been the one who died, and I agree; I should have lost my life when that demonic motherfucker pushed her down the stairs. She was always his favorite. Ollie was the sound of his heart.

"Let me live. I have no control over what happened to you when we were little. He made me suffer too. That motherfucker gave me a child!"

"I know, love. He told you that your son was God's gift. Funny how life works, my beautiful twin sister."

"Olivia, no! Don't you say that. What he did to me was no gift. Why didn't you help me?" I screamed from the back of my soul. I trembled at the thought of the little girl I once adored not reaching out to help me.

"You could have saved me, you cowardly bitch!" I yelled. "Come out of that fucking light and face me. Let yourself be seen. Show me I am not talking to myself. Show me I'm not a crazy bitch!"

"Hi, twin sister. Do you want to play a game?"

"What game, you little bitch?"

"You know the game. It's the pretend game, silly. The game where you pretend to be me and I pretend to be you; sort of like what we were doing in the mirror. You copycat me and I'll copycat you. The only catch is that I choose when it happens. Do you remember that game?"

"Olivia, I am so sorry. I didn't mean for that to happen, twin sis. I couldn't tell them you were the one that fell. It would have given away our secret and I would have lost the game. Pastor would have killed me."

"Yeah, he would have killed you. The same way he killed me, twin sister."

"Why didn't you save me from the monster, Olivia? You know he thought I was you."

"I know," she said.

The thought of that little bitch not helping me made my skin crawl. "That motherfucker told me what he put inside of me was God's little secret. Why didn't you keep your promise of being your sister's keeper?"

"It was revenge, twin sister; it was revenge because you never saved me from what Daddy did to me. He pushed me down the stairs because he thought I was you. Why didn't you help? Why weren't you your sister's keeper? Dear sweet Lydia never cared for anyone but herself."

"There's was no way for me to help you," I said.

"That's a lie! You could have saved me."

"How?"

"You could have killed him. Now, do you want to play a game? If you do, I'll need you to put on some clothes."

# CHAPTER 34

# TO DANCE WITH MOMMA

146

My momma always replaced her blues with the joy she got from hearing her favorite song on the stereo. She told me God secretly hid inside of music, and if I ever wanted to meet Him, all I had to do was turn on the radio and wait for the DJ to play one of my favorite records. I would never have to request a song. God knew the music written on my heart; I just had to close my eyes, take a deep breath, and wait for the radio to turn on. It would be a way of God telling me He was watching.

I looked up to the sky and wondered, *If I could trade places with God, would he even know I existed?* The man upstairs needed to prove that he cared, so I got down on my knees one night before I went to bed and prayed to the radio for a better life. I got as close as I could to the speaker and said my sincerest prayer:

"Now the light has gone away, Savior, listen while I pray. Asking Thee to watch and keep. And to send me quiet sleep. God, I want you to swear that you won't continue to allow my momma to weep. I want you to continue playing the songs she likes on the radio; it's the only thing that makes her happy. Can you please keep her from sticking needles in her arm? God, can you help us? Can you stop us from being poor? Can you stop the kids at school from laughing at me? They make fun of the way I dress. They talk about my momma too. I don't want us to be rich, I just want us to be better; I just want us to have the stuff we never had. God, can you play me a song on the radio so I know you're listening? I love you. Amen."

I took a deep breath and continued to keep my eyes closed. I waited for God to tell me something. He never played me a song on the radio. Nothing came through the speaker—not a single sound. For that reason, I hated music.

I hated the way my momma would get high and dance. She was good at doing an old school dance move from the mid-eighties called the wop, even though the Roger Rabbit was the thing happening back at the time. Momma was out of touch.

"Come. Let Momma show you how to cut a rug. Boo-key! Being a shy fly will never get you no girls." She grabbed my hand and led me out into the center of the ... floor. "Let me show you how to get the ladies, player!"

I pulled away. "I don't want to dance!"

She yanked me back toward her. "Don't let go of my hand, boy."

"I don't want to dance. Dancing is for stupid girls."

"No, son. Not dancing is for stupid boys. Are you a stupid boy, boo-key?"

"No, I am not. And stop calling me boo-key. I am not a baby anymore!"

"You are right, baby. My little book-book bear is not a cub anymore," she said.

A slow song poured out of the radio. The tune was a smooth R&B joint called *Just Me and You* by Tony, Toni, Tone. She pulled me back in closer, moving my hands back around her waist.

"Dance with me," she said.

As we danced slowly, she squeezed me tighter, pressing my body up against hers while kissing me on the cheek and giving me an awkward smooch on the lips. She tried to slip me the tongue. I was only nine years old. I pulled my face away before it was too late. She took my hands from around her waist and placed one of them on her breast. She took my other hand into hers, forcibly lowering it down onto her ample backside; making me palm one of her butt cheeks.

I quickly yanked my hands away. "Momma! What are you doing? Stop playing!"

"No one's playing, boy. Since you think you're so grown up, I figured you wouldn't have a problem with touching a woman's booty. You are a man, aren't you?"

I was shocked, sickened, and disturbed at the same time. I told her it wasn't right. She must have seen the disgusted look on my face.

She looked at me, sneering. "You don't even have any hair on your little dick, yet. Your stinky, booty, bird chest-having-ass, boy! Little motherfucker just barely stopped pissing on himself, thinking he's too much of a man to dance with his momma."

"Momma, stop ... That's not what I meant."

"I know what you meant, boy. I just don't want you to grow up and be a faggot like your Auntie Charlie. He thought girls were stupid too. Do you think I am a stupid girl?"

I knew she wasn't, even though she had a weird way of showing it. "No way, Jose. You are the prettiest girl in the world."

Momma blushed as tears filled her eyes. "I'm sorry," she said. "Dance with your momma, baby."

We hugged and danced. She sang a few words from the song on the radio. Something I said must have touched her heart. The way she felt was written all over her face. Her emotions started to run all over the place. She gently held both sides of my face in her calloused palms and kissed me softly on the forehead. She had the most beautiful chapped lips, the most striking soup coolers on our side of the Hyde Park. This was the closest I had ever felt to my mom. She leaned forward, bringing her face less than centimeters away from me, and then touching noses.

"The next time we dance, I want you to have some new moves," she said.

And that I did.

# CHAPTER 35

# ONION POUCH

"Go grab me an onion and that small leather pouch out of the refrigerator," Momma called out to me one day. "And I'm gonna need you to wash them dishes."

"Yes, ma'am."

I left my bedroom and headed toward the part of the house I hated the most—that nightmare of a kitchen. It was not only small and cluttered but infested with all manner of things that lived, breathed, and crawled on that disgusting surface we called a floor. We had dishes in the sink that were always stacked up higher than an elephant's eye. They were never a sight for sore eyes. I hated the way the faucet constantly dripped, and despised how the kitchen cabinets never closed all the way, no matter how hard you pushed them.

As I walked into the kitchen, I felt an enormous roach crawl onto my bare foot. I took my other foot and brushed it away as a stack of plates rattled in the cabinet above me. I looked up and saw a humongous rat running across the shelf of the cupboard. It was larger than any of the alley cats that lived near my building. When I saw it, I froze. I knew there would probably be a consequence if I had moved. Most rats' teeth were as sharp as razor blades. Momma said rats were the spawns of Satan. They all carried diseases and the souls of demons. If one of them ever bit you, you would turn into the child of the Devil.

I stayed still until the large rodent jumped from the cabinet and disappeared into another area of the kitchen. I grabbed the extremely large, ripened brown onion off the nearby counter. It was the size of a small cantaloupe, which wasn't the only thing that made it weird to look at, touch, or even feel, not to mention the fact it was heavy, sticky, and had a stench of burning pine. This wasn't just any type of onion. Supposedly, it was magic, and it came from the unknown jungles of West Guinea. Momma got it from the Hood Witch. I heard them talking about it when she brought it over. The onion was half vegetable, half spirit fruit. There was something inside it that could help my mom fight her drug problem. The Hood Witch said a shaman grew it. All Momma had to do was to put its juices inside her veins. Drinking it would never help, although I wished it could. I swiped the small leather pouch out of the refrigerator.

"Demetri, did you find it yet?"

"Yeah."

"Bring it in here."

I came back in and handed her the onion and pouch out of the refrigerator.

My mother took the onion, placed it on the table, and opened the pouch. She pulled out a hypodermic needle, a long piece of rubber tie strap, and a few other things I couldn't quite make out. She dumped the rest of the contents out onto the table. Momma took the strap and tied it around her bicep. She picked up the needle, which was the only regular part of the routine I ever saw her do. The onion was something different altogether.

"Go and get Momma a sharp knife, baby," she said.

"Okay," I responded. I ran into the kitchen.

She yelled after me, "Go in that drawer by the counter. Grab me that big knife with the brown handle on it."

"I got it!" I brought it back and handed it to her. Then stared at her, curious. "What are you doing?" I said.

"How many times do I have to tell you to stay out of grown folks' business?!"

I shrugged my shoulders. *I don't know. I'm hungry.* "Are you about to cook dinner? I saw a rat in the cabinet. I think it ate all the food."

"You already know Momma don't cook," she said.

"What do you need an onion for?"

"Boy, do me a favor. Go to your room."

"Okay."

She pointed at me with a stern warning before I left. "I don't want you peeking out here, okay. I don't want you exposed to none of this."

"Okay."

"I want you to remember I will always be by your side, son. Even when God is not there to answer your call, I want us both to find a better place. There is no future living here. We'll find a better way."

"What do you mean?" I said.

She stared at me with a hurt look, while she told me once again, "Go to your room."

From my bedroom door, I watched quietly as my momma fed her need. Despite how her facial features became spoiled from years of abuse, I noticed her overlooked beauty for the first time. Underneath her ashy, blemished skin, there was beautiful smooth skin waiting to be soothed and loved once again.

I stared at my momma, smiling. She glanced at me with a scowl. My grin dropped. My happiness disappeared. I pretended to shut the door, but I continued watching, and Momma continued to frown. She took the knife and split the onion into two halves. Momma set one-half of the onion aside and used the hypodermic needle to draw some juice from the other portion. She checked the needle's cc measurement as a parade of tears marched down her face. She gently wiped away the waterworks from off her cheeks in the same way a street sweeper sweetly brushes trash from off the streets. I could tell from her whimpers she was unaware I was watching.

"God help me," she said.

The universe didn't respond. Her chest rose as she took a deep breath. My upper frame did the same. I trembled with fear. Nerves danced up my arms and wrists.

She injected the onion-juiced hypodermic needle into her arm.

The onion extract had taken its effect. It caused Momma's body to tremble profusely. She gagged on her spit, foaming at the mouth. With so much saliva, she was like a hot pot on the stove boiling over with bubbling steamed milk that was destined to hit the floor. Her eyes rolled back into her head. Something was wrong. I had seen her get high before, but this time, it was more than one of her usual dope head junky fits.

"Momma, what's wrong?"

I headed over as she continued to convulse, rolling off the couch and onto the carpet. She gagged on saliva, gasping for air. Suddenly, her paroxysmal movement discontinued; she took another breath, lying motionless on the floor. I lay beside her, next to her, hugging her.

I remember pressing my head against my mother's chest, hoping to hear her heartbeat inside my eardrums once again, hoping she would wake up the side of my face. I lay against her breast for hours. Just then, hunger pains in my belly informed me it was way past time for my supper, so I went into the kitchen and fixed us two bowls of Cheerios—one bowl for my momma, and one bowl for me. I placed a dish of milky cereal next to her body, hoping she would join me for dinner once again. At the time, I was too young to realize my mother had died in front of my eyes, and that once a soul rises, the body it leaves behind never wakes. Her departed carcass would not have been useless. I would have cut away the bad parts.

# CHAPTER 36

# GLOWING AWAY PARTY

157

f I turned on the radio, I thought she might wake up. So, I headed over to the stereo and turned on some music. I looked up at the ceiling as if I was looking directly into heaven. I had a request for the man upstairs, "God, if you hear me, please allow Momma to wake up."

I stood there, waiting for music to start playing. There wasn't a single sound that came from the radio. I angrily yanked the stereo's electric cord from out of the wall, looked up at the ceiling, and told God to "go to hell!"

The apartment turned completely black; a bright glowing verve set alight inside Momma's corpse. The dials on the radio lit up, and a DJ's voice came through the speaker: "Coming up next is a classic by Nina Simone, *Don't Let Me Be Misunderstood.*"

The music started playing. As the slow, melodramatic tune played through the radio, my mother's corpse glowed brighter. A beam of light from the building's hallway crept inside the apartment from underneath the entrance door. The door slowly opened.

Momma's voice called my name. "Demetrius."

I knew it was something other than my mother calling me out into the hall. I looked back over at her body—it was gone.

The voice returned. "Come dance with your momma. I told you about being shy."

I followed her voice out into the hallway. She continued calling my name.

"Demetrius."

It was like the voice was repeating the thing my momma usually said to me growing up, and for that reason, I knew it wasn't my momma; I just knew it was something she wouldn't do, even if it were her returning from the other side.

The voice whispered behind me, egging me on, and I felt something over my shoulder.

"Peek-a-boo. I see you."

I turned around. No one was there. A door opened at the end of the hall. I heard my momma's voice coming from behind the bright light that led deeper into the room.

"Book-book bear, where are you?"

Looking back, I wondered what would have had happened if I never responded.

"I'm right here, Momma."

"Peek-a-boo. Now I see you. Come. Don't be scared. Walk toward The Light, my son."

I walked toward the room, and once I got close enough to step in, something emerged from out of the bright mass and yanked me in. The door slammed behind me.

"Where's my momma?" were the first words I said.

The Light responded in a deep, booming voice, "She wanted you to come to me."

"Are you God?"

"No, my child. I am not God. Consider me the greatest story the Bible never told."

I didn't know how to respond. There was only one question I could ask. "Am I dead?"

"No. You are chosen."

"Chosen?"

"There is something I need you to do."

"What do you want me to do?"

"I want you to live."

My mother's voice emerged from inside the Light. "I'm in a better place, Demetrius."

The girl's voice surfaced behind hers. "I'll make sure she's alright, Dee. She has a lot of family here that wants to see her."

The Light vanished.

* * *

When the paramedics came looking for my mother, I told them she was on the Other Side.

# CHAPTER 37

# LAST DANCE WITH MOMMA

I sat in the front row of my mother's funeral.

Pastor was fired up at my momma's memorial. He gave her eulogy to a church filled with funeral-goers and family members I'd never met.

"I loved my daughter, but God's children are not immune to the problems and trials of life."

A few older women in back of the church chimed in. "Amen! Amen, Reverend. Tell it like it is!"

"This is one of the hardest things I've ever had to do today—bury my daughter, my flesh and blood, as what is spirit is spirit. I can't determine what God decides to judge."

Granddaddy paused. Through his bifocals, I could sense the lump in the back of his throat. Choked up, he pushed himself forward to continue the sermon.

"I loved my daughter. Regardless of what I considered her to be, and of how ashamed I was of how she turned out to be." He took out a Bible from underneath the pulpit. "I want to recite a verse from 2 Corinthians 4:16-18:

"'Though outwardly we are wasting away, yet inwardly we are being renewed day by day. For our light and momentary troubles are achieving for us an eternal glory that far outweighs them all. So we fix our eyes not on what is seen, but on what is unseen. For what is seen is temporary, but what is unseen is eternal.'"

Granddaddy lifted his head, teary-eyed. "That same eternal light was inside my daughter, and the little boy she left behind is a little shining light of mine."

That was the first and last time I heard Pastor say something good about my momma.

Someone tapped me on the shoulder. I looked over and saw it was my momma. She was sitting next to me in the pew, wearing a white puffy dress. We both looked at each other, giggling like two school kids. My mother told me to take her hand as we both went up to the casket. She told me she was proud of me. Momma liked the fact I was being strong. She wanted to be there when I said my last goodbyes. We stood in front of her casket, hugging and smiling cheerfully, while everyone else cried.

"I thought I would never see you again," I said. "Can I ask you a question?"

"Sure, baby."

"Does God let you play the radio in heaven?"

"Yes."

My mother then took my hand and guided me up an aisle until we were at the center of the church. Suddenly, the pews of the funeral attendees disappeared. The room then dimmed, so it was just about dark enough to see what was going on. A spotlight appeared above me and my momma.

Music played through the church speakers. We were happy, and we started to dance.

EPILOGUE

# A NEW BEGINNING

*After my mother's death, my family household consisted of the six of us: my grandfather, my grandpa's religion, my granddaddy's relationship with his children, the passing of my grandma Mabel, that mysterious light in my room, and me.*

t was months after my mother died that I moved in with Pastor. I had hoped to move in with Auntie Charlene, but since my grandfather was a clergyman, who had money and a bigger house in a better neighborhood, it allowed him to claim me as a ward of the state. Auntie owned a boarding house in West Hollywood that housed a lot of runaway gay teens and young people, but some of them didn't have a clean enough record for me to live there—and neither did Charlene. My grandfather told me it was The Light that brought me there, but he also didn't want me living with my aunt. Unfortunately, living with Pastor was far from a blessing.

When I first moved there, I dreamed about funerals I would attend with my mother. In particular, I kept dreaming about seeing my father up close in a casket, with Momma always there to usher me down the aisle. In that dream, there was still a sad organ and people crying, dressed all in black. I didn't recognize anybody, but my mother in a white gown. She would come with me to the closed casket and tell me to open it, and as soon as  I got a look inside, I would see a man with a blank face. Then a blink of The Light blinded me and I woke in my bed, drenched in a cold sweat, and the radio alarm clock would go off—7 a.m. It was like it took me from out of my sleep to experience another dream, where a DJ's voice would blare through the speaker.

\* \* \*

"Good morning, it's time to rise and shine. This is your one and only DJ Galaxy, and I am bringing you your favorite jams from across the universe. Your mother says hello, Demetrius."

*What?* One of Momma's favorite tunes bled through the speakers. The jingle was *Ain't No Sunshine* by Bill Withers. I heard a knock at the door and went over to open it.

"Who is it?"

The door opened. A small body of light was sitting outside my bedroom.

I shouted once again, "Granddaddy?"

No one was there.

I heard a giggle.

"Hello?"

No response.

Suddenly, a shadow sped past my doorway. It moved quickly through the corridor, yet it remained within the massive brilliance. The silhouette resembled a shadow of a little girl who was running and playing inside the belly of The Light. Pastor yelled at the busy shadow from the other room. He wanted the shadow to stop running up and down the hall. Pastor sounded annoyed. He yelled at the young girl.

"Little girl, stop running in this dang, doggone hall. Don't make me warn you again."

"Dad, I'm trying to catch my ball! It won't stop rolling!"

"What did I bloody tell you about playing with that ball in this doggone house? If you want to mess around, go outside! That is what outside is for! Now do what I say!"

"Okay."

I walked through my bedroom door into the brightness. I headed toward the voices. The miniature sea of light vanished. I was now in the center of the foyer. Everything in the corridor was dim, except for that small spew of light that spilled from underneath the ingress of one bedroom farther up the hall at the opposite end of the passageway. From inside *that* room, a squeaky loose board creaked.

That room would later become a cryptic space—a not-so-quiet place. The chamber, which had sleeping quarters, had enough space for a hidden closet that led to where bodies were being buried, either dead or alive. That room was a special place filled with skeletons—the interred leftovers from unknown enigmas my momma never told me about. That room, coincidentally, was the place where my Grandma Mabel was last seen before she died, and where my granddaddy would never see his wife breathe again.

It was also the room next to where my granddaddy would rest his head and dream about the dead and even join them in another life again. That room was a place where my momma was badly beaten as a child, a space where my Auntie Charlene was trodden on for being a girl trapped inside a boy's body. That room, I should also point out, was the place where my momma conceived me when she was but a child herself. I wondered if the girl I saw in The Light knew that room for another reason.

Footsteps coming from that room pitter-pattered across that creaky loose board. *SQUEAK.*

"Hello?" I yelled up the hall.

The door to the room slowly opened, and a small red rubber ball came bouncing out. It slowly rolled towards me and stopped less than an inch away from my foot.

"Is anyone there?" I shouted again.

The little girl responded, "Depends who wants to know." There was not a soul in sight.

"I want to know." *Kind of? Sort of? Well, maybe.* "What are you doing in my granddaddy's house?" I said.

I recognized her as soon as she stepped out into the hallway wearing a puffy white dress with matching shoes, socks, and hair ribbons. It was the girl from The Light. She stood next to the childhood portrait of my mother and her twin sister on the nearby wall. She was the spitting image of them both. They were about nine, or maybe ten in that photograph. It looked like the same picture in my mother's photo album back home. I thought it was odd I didn't see the other twin. Maybe she was hiding.

Momma once told me a story about how, when she was little, Pastor would force her to wear long, puffy dresses with hair ribbons and shoes to match. She had a dress for each day of the week. He would call her Jesus's little princess. I wondered if this small bowl of a hot mess in a fancy dress could be Momma as a child. Or was it The Light fooling me? But how could that happen?

This little girl placed her sassy little hands on her slight hips. She had a whole world of feisty attitude waiting to get past her tiny lips. Jesus's small princess was an old soul with a look on her face that read, "I would kill you if it wouldn't mess up my dress. And, don't you dare touch one of my angel-colored ribbons. Do you understand the words coming out of my mouth?"

After a few more jeered facial expressions, she finally spoke. "Have you seen my sister?"

"No," I responded.

"No one can find her. She's been missing for a while," she said, looking sad and concerned.

"I hope she shows up. Do you want me to help you find her?"

"You don't live here. What are you doing in my daddy's house?" she said.

"I live here," I told her.

"Well, I live here too, and since this is my daddy's house, you need to go!"

I paused, trying to figure out the mystery of this smart-mouthed little girl. *You're the one that need to go.*

She rolled her little hazel eyes and her small neck.

*Cute? I don't think so.*

"Boy, what are you staring at? Have you ever seen a girl before?"

"Be quiet."

"Excuse me!"

*You're excused!* "What's up with that dress?"

"What is up with my dress?"

"I'm still trying to figure it out," I said.

Her jaw dropped. She was shocked. "Oh, no you didn't!"

*Oh, yes I did!* My grin let her know I knew I had gotten under her skin.

"Don't make me read you on a Sunday, boo-boo!"

"Today is Tuesday. Stupid!"

"Who are you calling stupid, fool!"

"I'm calling you stupid! STUPID! Looking a fool from head to toe. You and that dumb, stupid dress!"

"You look stupid standing in those dumb Spider-Man drawers and no shirt!

"Stupid!" *Shucks, she got me!* I had nothing else to say, except for, "I called you stupid first."

She knew she had me.

We stared at each other for a moment, checking each other out, up and down from foot to the noggin.

*Dang! That little girl, she has a big ole head.*

We read each other's facial expressions.

There was an awkward pause, and then we burst out in laughter.

*Wow! You are as silly as me. But for real, for real—who are you?*

What's your name?

"My name is Duncashane. What is your name?" she exclaimed.

"Duncashane! What's your name?" *I must beat you at your own little game.*

"Pooty Tang!"

"Pooty Tang?"

"Yep! If you ask me again, I will tell you the same!"

*Darn. She was good! But not good as me though.*

We both chuckled.

She looked at me and smiled.

*I have to know your name! Let's be friends.* "What's your name?"

She paused for a moment before responding, then told me softly, sweetly whispering, with a bit of reluctance in the back of her throat, "My name is Olivia, but you can call me Ollie for short."

*That's my momma's name.* "My name is Demetrius." I extended out a palm.

We shook hands.

She blushed.

I smiled. We had a weird connection. I pushed my words out gently. They blew past my lips like a kiss in the wind. "Nice to meet you," I softly expressed. I could tell she felt the same.

She looked me in the eye and whispered, "Nice to meet you, too."

*Why are you talking so low?* "Why are you whispering?" is what I said aloud.

"I don't want to wake my daddy," she said. "If you disturb him from his sleep, he gets very, very mean and angry. Once, I saw him get so mad he punched a hole through a wall and shook the house. You better run and hide if you ever awake him." Olivia pushed me away from the small red ball that was sitting near my foot in the corridor. She looked at me and smirked. "Do you like kickball?"

"Yeah, I guess so."

"Watch this."

She then kicked the red ball hard as she could up the hall, hitting and breaking a vase and knocking over a couple of small indoor pot plants. "BINGO!" she yelled.

We heard Pastor screaming at the top of his lungs. "What in Satan's burning hell is going on out there?" Pastor quickly came out of *that room* in his robe and pajamas. He had his pistol ready to go.

He saw me standing in the hall. "What are you doing out here, heathen? Thought somebody was breaking into my house."

"Sorry, Granddaddy. We were just playing."

Pastor looked at me like I was crazy. "What in doggone hell are you talking about, boy?"

"Me and Olivia!" I pointed over to Olivia. *She was involved in it, too.*

Olivia shrugged her shoulders, looked at me, and smiled. She egged on the torture. "It wasn't me, Daddy. I had nothing to do with this. It was him. He kicked the ball."

"Are you playing games with me, boy? Ain't nobody over there." Pastor slapped me across the face.

I fell to the floor, crying. He stood over me, looking down at me. I saw fire and brimstone in his eyes. The hammer of his gun was still cocked. I could tell he wanted to kill me. To do the job, all he had to do was point the pistol. I would have died from the shock of the moment; there wouldn't have been a need to fire his gun. He gave me the biggest scare of my life.

He leaned over, lowering himself downward, closer to me. "I'm going to tell your stupid little heathen tail this one time, boy. Don't you ever, in your good for-nothing, sorry excuse for a life, play games with me like you lost your doggone mind. Your momma wasn't nothing but an embarrassment to this family. She got on that narcotic and messed around and got herself pregnant with a little junkie baby. I took you in because I felt sorry for you. Prove to me that you are better than your momma, or I might find a reason for you to never have to prove anything to me, again! If it wasn't for God, I would have let your little butt go to the welfare."

Pastor leaned over, getting more in my face. "Take your mischievous self back to sleep. You have Bible study in a couple of hours. I'm going to make a righteous Christian out of you, even if it kills me." Pastor headed back to *that room*.

I looked over to see if Olivia was still there, but she was gone. I then headed back to my room to get some sleep.

*FLASH!*

Suddenly, a blink of bright light threw blackness in front of me before a body of brilliance laid before my eyes—an amazing depth of radiance flanked by a beautiful horizon filled with a collapsing, discharged galaxy. As its cosmos started to twirl, swirling like a whirlwind, it sucked the ocean of light into its black hole. Just then, I heard a voice from the heavens.

*You must not allow darkness to overcome you.*

*FLASH!*

I awoke in a cold sweat just as Pastor burst into my room.

"Boy, you need to get ready! You have a meeting with Jesus this morning!" Pastor slammed the door.

I pinched myself to see if I really was awake this time. I heard a voice in the corner of the room. It was Ollie, who had been standing there the entire time.

"You are not dreaming! Get dressed!"

"Why did you get me in trouble?"

She giggled.

I was flustered. *I wish you would stop chuckling!* "It wasn't that funny."

"You were scared."

"No, I wasn't."

Olivia stopped laughing. Her eyes went blank. She looked at me as if she'd seen a ghost. *Maybe she's the one that's afraid.*

"If you weren't scared, you should've been."

She had an eerie look on her face.

"Do you want to see something creepy?"

"Yeah." I was slow to respond.

"Meet us in Pastor's bedroom. Tonight, after he goes to sleep."

* * *

There was an area of Pastor's house I referred to as *that room*, which served as his private space. In that room, after his Bible studies, granddaddy would pour himself a spot of that brown stuff he kept in a flask that was always concealed in a special area of his Bible that he carved out himself. My momma said the flask was the reason he carried two Bibles. One of those Bibles taught the sayings of Jesus, while the other Bible held my granddaddy's liquid spirits, which were preferably liquor souls in the form of either Hennessey or Jack Daniels. My mother said that before Grandma Mabel died, she always joked with my granddaddy about the secret love affair he had with his closet whiskey. *That room* was the only place Pastor would allow himself to get piss drunk.

My mother said no one was allowed in *that room*, except for him and all those people that my momma said she never saw coming back out. However, Olivia and I would ironically become an exception. I still remember the breath of her whisper. She gently blew what she had to say into my ear.

"Wake up. He's asleep." She motioned me to get out of bed. "Come on. Get up."

She ordered me to be quiet, throwing a hush sign in front of her lips, and we tiptoed down the candlelit foyer.

*I'm cold.* "I need my jacket." *This is scary. I want to go back to my room.*

"Don't be a wuss," she said. "We're almost there."

"Once we're inside, you'll feel better. I promise."

Knowing now what I didn't know back then, I shouldn't have believed a word she said. The day I witnessed my mother's death would soon no longer be the worst day of my life.

We saw Pastor on the nearby couch sleeping. My granddaddy snored so loud that it reminded me of the sound bears make when they farted alone in the woods, minus the poop smell.

Olivia pointed to a bookshelf over in the nearby study. "We have to move that out of the way. There's a door behind it."

"What kind of door? What does it lead to?"

"You'll see. Just keep your voice down. I don't want my daddy to hear you."

"Okay."

Olivia struggled to move the humongous shelf on her own. She motioned me over. "Help."

I grabbed the other end and clued her in on what to do. "I push. You pull."

"Got it!" she whispered.

*I have an idea.* "Let's do it, on the count of three. One." *Don't dare push like a girl.* "Two." *This thing is heavier than the both of us put together.* "Three." *Pull!*

I pushed.

She pulled.

We pushed and pulled with all of our might.

*This!*
*Thing!*
*Won't!*
*Budge!*
*Doesn't!*
*Matter!*
*How!*
*Hard!*
*We!*
*Try!*

*I give up!* I threw my hands in the air. "This thing is too heavy."

"No, it's not. Keep pushing."

She didn't want to stop; she wanted me to continue. "We need to keep trying."

"We tried already." *I'm all tried out!*

"Don't be a chicken."

"I'm not scared," I said.

"We've got to try harder."

*Dang. She's a tough little cookie.* "Let's try harder next time." *Maybe then we'll be ready.*

"No!" she exclaimed. "Let's try harder now." And that's when I saw the light bulb above her head come on. Her eyes grew as wide as the pools of The Light, and she told me her bright idea. "Let's push the shelf from your side."

"My side?" *The heavier side?*

"Yeah! Your side, stupid." She was annoyed, but not quite annoyed as I was.

*She seems to always have this snarky little neck roll every time I say something she doesn't agree with. I don't understand. Why's she have to be so sassy? Who's going to pull the weight of the shelf from the other end?* I wasn't quite sure, so I asked her, "Don't we need someone to tug from the other side?"

She rolled her eyes, "No!"

*Her response was so rude.*

"Neither one of us needs to tug, stupid," she answered impolitely. She sighed in disgust. Olivia was annoyed and she didn't mind telling me. "Stupid, stupid, stupid little boy!" She reinforced her insult with a snarl.

"Stop calling me stupid!" I said. "I just want to know what we are going to do if it falls and makes noise."

"Don't worry. It won't fall if we don't flip it over. Scaredy chicken." She moved over to my side of the shelf. "Let's put both of our backs up against this thing."

"Okay." *I guess. It seems like a good idea. It may work out.*

She prompted me on what to do next. "We're going to count it out, the same way we did before, but this time I'm doing the count. So one ... two ... three?" She gave me a look. "You got it?"

*What you got to lose?* "Roger that," I said. *It's a simple enough plan. STOP CALLING ME STUPID! If you knew how loud I am screaming inside myself, you wouldn't keep calling me stupid. I am no one's scaredy chicken. You better stop calling me names, or else.* And that's when I looked over and saw her expression that said, *Or else what?* I kept what I had to say to myself. I just glared at her vacantly.

She sighed in frustration. "What are you looking at?" she said. "We're going to count out like before, but this time I'm doing the count."

"Okay."

"Ready?" she prompted.

I nodded. *Yes.*

Her face dropped.

"Answer me when I ask you a question."

*Oh boy. The feisty one's mouth grew even bigger.*

"You need to open up your mouth and speak out any of the words that you need to say to me. Use your vocabulary. Hasn't your mother taught you how to speak?"

I shrugged my shoulders and responded in my head. *No. She is dead. She isn't around to teach me anymore.* I nervously put my thumb in my mouth and stared at Olivia blankly, watching her reactions. She was clearly ticked off about me not responding.

"You're still just going to stand there? Answer me back!"

*I already did.*

She snapped her fingers in my face, shouting, "Hello! Anyone there?" She called out to me, putting her hands on her hips, rolling her neck. "Say something!"

"I did say something. You didn't hear me." *Okay, that came out well.*

"What are we doing? Answering people without saying words now?"

"I guess."

"Yeah, I guessed right. You are a chicken," she said.

"I am not a chicken," I stressed.

Granddaddy must have heard me. I looked over at the couch and saw him move a little in his sleep. Ollie wouldn't keep quiet. I wasn't about to answer another one of her questions. *So I thought.*

"You think I am boo-boo the fool?"

"No," *but you look like him.* "I didn't say that," *out loud at least. Dang. Here it comes. I'm about to get an earful. Somebody! Anybody! Please! Just shoot me in the head.*

"Why did Jesus make me a Christian? Lord knows you get on my nerves. You are such a frigging mess. We will work on making you a better you—later. Life is too short, and neither one of us has as much time as God. You really know how to put somebody's underclothes in a bunch. I tell you."

*What?* "Can we please just push this thing before Pastor wakes up?" I asked.

"Ding goes the bell," she mockingly said. "That's why we're here! Somebody give a prize to the boy with the big, giant water head. I am so glad you figured out our purpose. Can somebody give a gold star to Demetrius? He is really, truly, amazingly smarter than he looks. I mean that in the sincerest, kindest, and oh-so-loving way."

*You a smarty pants! I hate your mouth.* "Let's push the shelf," I said.

"Yes, sir!" Olivia said. She was still mocking me. "Be sure to push the shelf like a rooster, not a chicken. Roosters are bigger and stronger," she claimed.

I looked over on the couch. Pastor was still asleep. It was a good time to try again. We counted to three and pushed the humongous shelf as hard as we could. The shelf started to budge. It rocked back and forth, but didn't move far enough to get any leeway. The large silver urn on top of the mantle tilted as if it would topple over.

 XXVI

Olivia was the first to stop pushing. She pointed to the mantle. "The urn! Catch it before it falls!"

I dashed over in front of the shelf. I was too short to stand on my tiptoes and push the vase back in its place. Since the shelf was too heavy for me to hold still, I did the next best thing. I cupped both of my hands and held them out underneath the vase, anticipating that the shelf's rocking would knock over the urn. I was hoping to catch whatever I could whenever it fell. I needed Olivia to have my back and hissed for her to come in front of the shelf next to me.

"I need your help! Help me catch the urn."

Olivia didn't budge. She stood frozen. "You got it!" she moaned.

The shelf kept rocking.

It was well on its way to falling over until I saw a large brown hand reach from behind me and grab the shelf. Someone was helping me to hold the mantle sturdy; too bad they weren't quick enough to catch the urn before it fell. The urn tipped over, and I ended up with two palm loads full of ashes in my hand. *Whose ashes were they?*

I looked over to Olivia. She was gone. She was nowhere in sight. I looked over at the couch to see if Pastor was sleeping. He wasn't there. I turned around to see who was behind me, helping me hold up the shelf. It was Pastor. His giant frame was standing behind me.

His glare came down like the wrath of God. "What in the world are you doing in my room, heathen?"

I was too scared to respond. I could tell he sensed my fear; it was oozing through my aura. I knew a horror was about to happen.

"You're sticking your nose in places where it doesn't belong, boy!"

*Am I about to die? Think fast!* And so I did. I came up with a lie. "I was trying to stop the shelf from falling over. I didn't want to wake you." *How honest did that sound? I wonder if he bought it. Is Pastor going to believe my lie?*

He stared at me as if he knew I was up to something. "Who you fooling, heathen?! You are dealing with a coon wiser than Methuselah. No need to tiptoe around the Pearly Gates if you're not ready to go in," he advised.

*What does that mean?*

"What you doing in my room, heathen?"

"Nothing."

"That's what Judas told Jesus."

*That was weird and creepy! Are you threatening to put me on the cross?* "You are scaring me," I said. *You are really freaking me out!* I took a couple steps away from him.

He saw me moving and stopped me in my tracks. "Where you going, boy? You're not getting out of this!"

I could tell he didn't want me to pull away and pondered what to do to me. From the way he glared and licked his teeth, I knew I had trouble.

His room was a jungle. Pastor was a lion licking his teeth before a feast. He was a monster prepared for the kill. He was a hungry beast. I was a lion's meal. My fear was its feast. My momma said Granddaddy always licked his teeth when he was angry, so I had to watch out. Pastor was pissed. His anger allowed him to force out words.

"Don't be scared. If you were up to nothing, you shouldn't be afraid."

*But I am afraid.* My body trembled as he stepped closer to me.

When he stared me in the eyes, I saw that his face was dead. His emotions were lifeless. He had the personality of a ghost. Then Pastor looked down and saw that I was still holding the ashes from the urn in my hands. I'd been holding the ashes the entire time.

"How much do you know about life to hold someone's death in your hand? How much you doggone know, you little heathen? Do you even know how to respect death? Do you even know how those ashes got in that urn, boy?"

I shrugged my shoulders. "Is it something my momma put there?"

"Poor child. Those ashes you are holding belong to Ben."

"Who is Ben?" I asked.

He took a long, awkward pause before responding, pondering what to say. "Ben was my best friend," he said.

The life in his eyes told me he wanted to tell me something. *Hopefully a secret?*

There, on the couch, was where he told me a story about how Ben was his pet dog when he was a boy around my age. Pastor then told me not to go poking around in his room again and said I needed to "get some shut eye."

Once I got back inside my room, I cut off the lights and got ready for bed.

Ollie was there, looking worried. "We need to get back inside that room, Demetrius. Please. Don't let what he told you about those ashes fool you. That room has a secret basement. Just go through the door behind the shelf. He's hiding my sister and mother's bodies somewhere inside. I know they're dead. It's been a long time since I saw them and Charlie ran away. He can't help us."

"I'm too small to do anything. Can we call the police?"

"They won't believe you," Ollie said with a haunted look on her face. "But we'll be back to tell you what to do when the time comes. Be strong—The Light is always in you. Pastor's darkness has too much control over him."

As I climbed into bed and turned off my lamp, getting under the covers, Ollie kissed me on the forehead as she tucked me in—something my mother used to do.

"Get some sleep, boy. You have church in the morning."

"Yes, ma'am."

"Don't call me ma'am; it makes me feel old."

My bedroom door slowly opened to reveal The Light, which had a silhouette of a large, elderly woman who looked like my great-great Irish grandma Cindy. She was standing in the brilliance of radiance outside my bedroom door. Ollie slowly pulled away and headed toward the silhouette standing inside The Light, who was waiting for her to walk out.

I watched as Ollie hugged the silhouette and turned into an equally dark shadow. "I love you, Great Granny," she told the woman.

"Are you not a sweet apple," Cindy replied. "I love you a lot more, me pretty. Thee boy, does he know what to do?"

"Not now, Granny, but he will."

I saw their shapes transform into orbs and disappear before The Light faded away. Then I heard an alarm ring. There was a blink of light. I woke up sweating, trying to catch my breath. The clock nearby read 7 a.m., and the radio turned on with another one of my mother's favorite old school jams.

Pastor yelled from the hall, "Boy, get up and take a bath. We have to get to church this morning."

Lightning Source UK Ltd.
Milton Keynes UK
UKHW040637230522
403330UK00012B/5